Tropic Of Scorpio
Robert Perchan

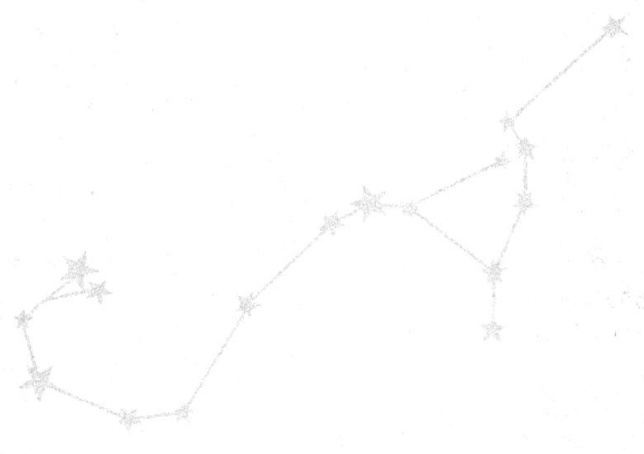

SPUYTEN DUYVIL

New York City

ACKNOWLEDGMENTS

The passage beginning *I didn't hear the water running* and ending *what we do for them* originally appeared in *Erotic Review* (ermagazine.com, October 6, 2021) under the title "Give Piss a Chance."

The six word stories scrawled on the men's room wall in Chapter XII originally appeared in *Rat's Ass Review* (Winter 2020) under the title "13 Ways of Looking at a Six Word Story."

The passage beginning *I guess you are all wondering* and ending *I'm really fucking DEAD!* originally appeared under the title "On My New S.O.D. Card" in the anthology *It's About Time* (Main Street Rag Publishing Company, Charlotte, N.C., 2016)

© 2022 Robert Perchan
ISBN 978-1-956005-81-3

Library of Congress Cataloging-in-Publication Data

Names: Perchan, Robert, 1947- author.
Title: Tropic of scorpio / Robert Perchan.
Description: New York City : Spuyten Duyvil, [2022]
Identifiers: LCCN 2022038682 | ISBN 9781956005813 (paperback)
Classification: LCC PS3566.E68 T76 2022 | DDC 813/.54--dc22
LC record available at https://lccn.loc.gov/2022038682

It is—or seems to be—a wise sort of thing, to realise that all that happens to a man in this life is only by way of a joke, especially his misfortunes, if he have them. And it is also worth bearing in mind, that the joke is passed around pretty liberally & impartially, so that not very many are entitled to fancy that they in particular are getting the worst of it.

Melville

Now with the advent of biotechnology we are facing a possibility—it's not a prophecy, it's not certain—but there is a possibility of real biological gaps opening and *Homo sapiens* splitting into different biological castes—or even different species.

Yuval Noah Harari

I.

I was sitting quietly in my living room with the windows of the bungalow open to the early October tropical island breeze and Fatal Encounters on tv when the airship began its slow descent over the parking lot of the Long Pig ribs joint across the street. It hovered there for a few minutes and then a door opened in the gondola of the thing and a sort of escalator extruded down and almost touched the surface of the asphalt. No handrails. Just the stairs. Soon enough an Alien figure in a black and orange Hazmat suit appeared and glided down the steps. It entered the pork ribs joint and the airship lifted off and vanished in the growing dark.

I was not long off the phone with McPheeters at the Long Pig when the doorbell rang.

It was the Alien. With a white paper carry-out bag gripped in an oversize Hazmat glove.

"I have a few questions," the Alien hissed. "We are taking a little census of the neighborhood."

"Sure," I said. "Go ahead, Alien. Shoot. Everybody knows you're not for real. Everybody knows who you work for."

"I don't want to hurt you," the Alien hissed at me. "Nobody's shooting anybody. Even if you clowns are goofball enough to call us Aliens." Its voice was scratchy but nonetheless clear.

"Okay," I said. "Fair enough."

"What was your mother's maiden name?"

I answered complaisantly. I did not yet see where this was going.

"And your first pet's name?"

I told the Alien I had never had a pet. Ever. Unless you counted the iguanas that hung out on the terrace.

"I see," the Alien hissed. "No. We won't count the iguanas."

"They're everywhere. Just staring and staring."

"Sure. And the name of the kid who bullied you in grade school?"

I told the Alien the name of the little prick. You are not supposed to remember this crap but you do just the same.

"Okay. Good. That sounds about right," the Alien hissed. "And the name of the last woman you had sex with?"

"I don't remember," I said.

"Don't fuck with me on this one," the Alien hissed menacingly. Still scratchy but menacing just the same.

"It was a long time ago," I said.

"Try again," the Alien hissed. "We just want to identify your level of verity."

"Justine?"

"Hmm. Take your time. We want to get this one right."

"Yumi?"

"You sure?" the Alien hissed. It did not sound pleased.

"Not exactly."

"Look, everybody remembers the last person they had sex with. *Everybody*."

"Okay, Justine. I'm sticking with Justine."

"That's better. Much better. Now," the Alien hesitated a little, "may I use your bathroom?"

What could I say? What would *you* say?

"Through the kitchen," I said. "And to the left."

The Alien found the bathroom like it knew exactly where it was going. I do not think it even flicked on the light. I heard the water running in the tub. Christ, I thought. Is the damned thing going to take a bath? Then the toilet flushed and the tap water stopped running.

The Alien came back into the living room. Its Hazmat suit was unfastened a hitch at the top now.

"You're going to catch your death," I said. "Or whatever you things catch. In *War of the Worlds* the Martians—"

"Oh shut up, Harold," the Alien hissed. "We're not like you and we don't *catch* stuff. We have antibodies you would give your left ball for."

The Alien knew my name! Had I given it earlier? No, I was sure I had not.

"Now, Harold," the Alien hissed on. "As to your political affiliations. On a scale of one to ten—ten being the strongest—how would you rate—"

"*Mother!*" I shouted at the door of the spare bedroom that had no bed in it. "There's an Alien here and it's asking—"

"Jesus Christ!" the Alien roared scratchily. "Don't tell me you *still* tell people you still live with your MOTHER?"

"Well," I said. The "mother" business was a ruse, of course. The Alien was right. I used it all the time to keep people from getting too close. And I did not want the Alien to think I was all alone now. I did not trust the menace in that hiss.

"I'll bet," the Alien hazarded scratchily, "you like to fuck women doggy style too. So you don't get them pregnant.

Bend them over the back of that there armchair and have at them from behind like your troglodyte ancestors. Then pull out before it's too late. When your 'mother' is out at Bingo. Isn't that right, Harold? Isn't that exactly right?"

My eyes narrowed in fury. "Justine," I snapped. "Is that you inside that damned spaceman getup?"

I made to thrust my hand inside the unfastened flap of the Hazmat suit. I expected to come upon Justine's breast inside there—her squooshy boob with its rubbery aureole. But it was blocked inside. I had no idea how such suits worked. I groped around a little further but it was like my hand was inside an empty pocket. Dead end. Blind.

"Satisfied now?" the Alien hissed. "Shall we continue?"

"I don't think I like where all this is going," I whined. "That's all."

"Just keep your hands to yourself. Now on a scale of one to ten—ten being the strongest—what do you think of Clinton's chances in next month's election?"

"Clinton," I gasped. "Zero," I said. "Zilch. Hasn't the world FINALLY had enough of the Clintons!"

"Okay," the Alien hissed. "Of course. I was just testing you. Now this Justine that you mentioned."

"She's my ex-girlfriend. Leave her out of this."

"She disappeared this past June. Is that not correct?"

"She was an unhappy woman," I explained.

"Oh?"

"The botched boob job."

"I see."

"Our career stalled by the Crash."

"And?"

"So I cut her loose."

The Alien tapped its big Hazmat suit boot impatiently.

"She had more talent than me. She was better off on her own."

"That's better," the Alien hissed sympathetically. "Now we're getting somewhere."

"And there was this Asian chick I was fooling around with. Behind her back—"

"You little RAT! Talking about that to a stranger!"

"I know. But it didn't last. It was just a fling. And then there was the abor-"

"Okay. Fine," the Alien hissed flatly, peremptorily.

"-tion. I don't think she—"

"Enough, Harold!"

"—ever got over that. I took her to Europe just to comp—"

"*ENOUGH!*" the Alien screeched scratchily, and I rocked back on my heels. "You've said enough. You've fessed up. Now, would you like to bring her back?"

"Pardon?"

"Would you like to bring her back?"

"She's long gone. Like you said."

"But you thought I was her. You called out her name and tried to stick your hand inside my suit."

"They never found a body. Just her clothes on the beach. The crazy night after the Summer Solstice party at the Patio."

"So you believe she might still be alive?"

"I didn't mean for her to disappear like that," I moaned.

"What would you give to bring her back?"

"Give?" I said.

"To see her in the flesh once again?"

"Shit," I whined again. "I'd give almost anything. I never meant—"

"This island?" the Alien hissed.

"Pardon," I said.

"This island. This little pisshole of a tropical paradise you call home. Would you give that up?"

"It's all I have," I said. "I don't have anywhere else."

"I knew you would say that, butt brain. Why the hell do you think I am here?"

"I don't have anyplace to go back to. Everybody knows that. I'm not like the others. They're young enough they can just pack up and—"

"Harold!" it hissed.

"You can't kick *everybody* off—"

"For Justine! For sweet young Justine—who gave up *everything* for you!"

"Okay," I said. "Sure," I said. It was easy enough to lie to a creature in a Hazmat suit. No eye contact and all that. "In a heartbeat. Why not. And I think Chelsea will win in a landslide next month too. In a tsunami!"

"Jolly good," the Alien hissed. "Jolly jolly good. Now all you have to do is keep your word."

"Justine," I wept bitterly, inconsolably—and I hoped convincingly—whatever game was being played. "I love you and I want you back again. Wherever you are."

"Okay," the Alien hissed. "That will do. Enough of the Mrs. Calabash. Don't overdo it. And here's some ribs for you, motherfucker. Just the way you like them. Angus says Hello."

II.

"**D**oes this thing work? Do you still get satellite?" The Alien had picked up the remote and was jabbing it in the direction of the tv set.

"Okay," it hissed. "There it is."

"Where's Justine?" I snapped.

"Do you get the History Is Bunk Channel now? I love Ancient Aliens. Especially the Sheela Na Gig Cenote Episode."

"When is Justine going to get here? You promised."

"Rome wasn't built in a day, Harold."

"Justine," I insisted. "Where is she?"

The Alien sat down on the sofa with a sort of hissing grunt. For the first time I noticed its knees and waist and elbows were creased and wrinkled like the Hazmat suit was a couple of sizes too big for it. Normally I detest shabbiness in strangers but my pity was aroused. Here was a creature suited up like it was from some distant world and it could not even afford a decent fitting set of space duds. I imagined if it had a pet back on Planet Zed it probably looked like one of those chupacabras cryptozoids—like a coyote with the mange. I imagined its mother slaving away behind the counter of some interstellar greasy spoon. Hell, maybe the damned thing was just taking a break from scrounging around in some cosmic dumpster.

"Don't look at me like that," the Alien hissed.

"Like what?"

"You know nothing about me."

"This is not about you. This is about Justine."

"I'm not just a Brain in a Vat, you know."

The Alien had found the Comedy Channel. There I was on tv again. My Josephine and Napoleon routine. They ran it at the end of the hour once in a while when they needed five minutes of filler. Even the station manager owned I was pretty good—for a one trick pony. Standup is hard. Like spanking the iguana, Angry Stan once quipped, on a streetcorner in front of a crowd. You are never so alone as you are up on stage. And yet you are the center of the universe too.

"Turn that off," I said.

"That's you," the Alien hissed.

"Change the channel."

"No. I've got to see this. I never saw this one."

Did you see the WWN News report a while back—about a drunken male college student out in California who was arrested for breaking into a university animal husbandry unit and having sex with a SHEEP.

"Lame, Harold," the Alien hissed. "Weak. Sex with sheep jokes."

"It's an old story. From way back. I dug it up this past summer and we vid—"

"Was this kid you? You never told—"

"Hey," I said.

NON-CONSENSUAL SEX, according to the Arresting Officer. Now there was no evidence that the kid used a DATE RAPE DRUG or anything like that.

"Love that stuff," the Alien hissed. "Gamma-hydroxybutyrate. You got any?"

"Jesus, what the fuck sort of Halloween planet are you supposed to be from tonight?"

"Had you going there, didn't I, Hare Oil."

"Hare Oil! Justine! I knew it!"

"Shh. Not my name. Sorry."

The kid was NO BILL COSBY.

"Who's Bill Crosby?"

"A disgraced comedian. Blackballed. Long time ago."

"Like you?"

"I wasn't blackballed. It was a generation thing. I wasn't generating enough laughs—"

On the other hand, it was clear that he did not understand the meaning of the word BA-A. I don't know—maybe you can't blame him for misunderstanding. I mean if you have ever seen a big flock of sheep all packed into a tiny little pen and all of them going BA-A BA-A—well it's pretty clear that BA-A really means HEY GET YOUR FACE OUT OF MY ASS OKAY.

"Not bad," the Alien hissed approvingly. "That's how they say it is on an airship sometimes. On holiday runs anyhow."

Later on in the report, the WWN reporter asked this husky young coed at the school animal husbandry lab—a real 4 H Club farmer's daughter type, I might add—the reporter asked her what she thought of the whole thing. She pronounced it DISGUSTING. JUST DISGUSTING.

"Farmer's daughter. I adore farmer's daughter jokes. It is said Freud knew more than seven hundred of them. Bergson claimed—"

"Enough," I shot back. "There's nothing drearier than theor—"

"Shush," the Alien hissed.

Then the reporter asked her Well, what do you do with the sheep here anyways? Why are you keeping sheep here in the first place? And the animal husbandry girl said, Oh, we BREED them.

The Alien stared at the screen, transfixed. I lunged for the remote but the Alien jerked it away.

"Keep your hands to yourself, Harold. So grabby."

In other words, if a SHEEP and a RAM don't want to have anything to do with each other—if they just want to go their own way and do their own thing—it's okay to force them to have sex. To COPULATE. It doesn't matter if they are NOT INTERESTED in each other. It doesn't matter if they have OTHER IDEAS.

"Mutual consent," the Alien hissed. "Free will. What a bloody joke."

"Heavy," I said.

"To each his or her own," the Alien hissed and shrugged wearily.

"Huh," I said.

It's okay to say to the sheep, JOSEPHINE, we really don't give a shit what you want. JOSEPHINE—that's not her real name. I just made that up. The University wouldn't release the sheep's real name. That's their policy. Sheep deserve protection—at least until jiggy jiggy animal husbandry insemination time rolls around.

"Jiggy jiggy insemination time," the Alien hissed. "Nice touch that. Effective juxtaposition of the vulgar with the clinical. Dick Brain."

"Your approval is duly noted. Clit Lisp."

"Nice," it hissed. Or maybe it was "nithe". I could not tell.

So it's okay to say to the sheep, JOSEPHINE, we really don't care what you want. Get your YANGBOJI over here and present it to Napoleon. YANGBOJI is Korean for sheep's vagina. I just thought I'd throw that in MY vagina monologue. I think STAND UP COMEDY ought to be educational as well as entertaining. Josephine, get your YANGBOJI over here. This is for SCIENCE.

"You speak Korean," the Alien hissed. "Did you learn it from that Yuki slut?"

"Yumi. And it was just a fling. I learned a little Korean on the—"

"Shush. We know all about that."

And Napoleon, you get your sorry excuse for a ram's pecker over here pronto and have at this sheep bitch. We don't care if you prefer other rams—or even LITTLE LAMBSIE DIVIES. We don't give a damn what your preferences are. This is for SCIENCE.

"Little Lambsie Divies. I loved their White Album!"

"Weak, Justine. Weak."

"Not my name. Guess again."

But if one of the partners is a drunken male college student— and he's more than willing to tup poor Josephine up—then it's wrong. Then it's immoral. Disgusting. Even illegal. Then it's BA-A-AD.

"You do a tolerable sheep's bleat, Harold," the Alien hissed. "You sure you're not a hybrid?"

"*You* tell *me* something. You sure you're not one of those

Aliens that goes around abducting people and doing weird shit to their reproductive tracts?"

"That's putting it rather crudely, Harold."

Now here's the best part. Absolutely the best part. And this is absolutely true. At the end of the news report, the reporter asked the animal husbandry gal how the sheep was doing now—how the sheep was coping with all the trauma and attention now—and the girl said the sheep is being TREATED for the incident. I don't know what that means exactly—but I suspect that in California Speak it means the sheep is now in THERAPY.

"Therapy," the Alien hissed. "Love that. Hand jobs for the homely and the lonely! Do you still pop in the Happy Ending now and again?"

"I don't think that's any—"

"How's Rudolfa?"

The screen went blank for a second and then a fifty year old Seinfeld rerun was on the air. It was the top of the hour. My Therapy Session send up riff was scrubbed. It was the one part of the routine I still stood by.

The Alien stood up and walked over to the window and flung it open. Its chest heaved as if it were taking a deep breath.

"God," it hissed. "I love the smell of pork ribs in the evening. Remember our first date at the Long Pig?"

"Justine!" I cried. "I knew it!"

And then:

"There's Stavros and the Ganymede. There's my ride!"

III

In the morning I walked to the office. I passed the Long Pig and looked in the big window. There was no one there. The restaurant was not yet open. Behind the glass door of the big cooler three slabs of pork ribs hung on hooks. Indeed they looked cool to the touch. Some blocks further down I crossed the little footbridge over the canal. A gondola drifted underneath. Its gondolier leaned on his oar, asleep. I envied him his ease. I asked him once if he knew any gondola jokes and he told one about anal sex. I didn't see the connection and when I told him so he just stared at me. Later on Justine explained it to me. I still did not get it. You have no imagination, Harold, she said. Then I told it to some of my friends, and they laughed hilariously. They even slapped me on the back. Harold, they howled. Where do you come up with this stuff?

In the office my assistant was out at her barista lesson so I had to make coffee myself. I had taken her on as a sort of scholarship interne and gave her a little pocket money now and again. The barista lessons was her way of hinting that she deserved a real salary, I suppose. Or maybe like so many others she was just looking ahead at an uncertain future. Miss Soobiah did not do much except water the plants and keep the attendance and financial records but she seemed convinced that her presence at her desk improved the image of the place. Her breasts jiggled as she tapped at the keyboard, at any rate. I told her once that if she wanted to make it as a comedian she needed to come up with some good boob jokes. This miffed her. She was not going to use her body to launch a career on stage. Just to get you started, I said. You can drop them later. You mean after they start to sag, she snapped coolly.

Some students had gathered in the room down the hall. It was top of the hour. I slapped my notes together to meet them. McPheeters was at his desk in his office as I walked by. His holstered gun hung by a shoulder strap from the coat rack beside his tam o' shanter. I looked in.

"Knock knock," I said.

He got up from his swivel chair and came to the door and shut it. He was not a morning person, he told me once, but I liked to test him.

In the classroom there was a nervous hum about the field trip on Saturday night. We were down to four people in the Advanced Class and I felt confident everyone would take a shot at the Open Mike. Sure, I was a little worried about Mr. Kang. He was a North Korean refugee and knew about forty different rice jokes, but none of them made any sense in English. Outside of the starving villagers in Africa on tv, Mr. Kang was the hungriest looking person I had ever seen in my life. It was not just his sunken cheeks. It was in his eyes. When they swept a room, it was as if he was scanning it for prey. At any rate, it was not wise to let them get carried away with apprehensions about mike fright. Better to ease them into the first exercise of the morning.

"So the Buddha walks into this bar," I began.

"And the bartender says—" Ms Grabor-Hepinstall added wearily.

A long pause. The road was forking. Mr. Kang tensed in his chair like he was straining at stool. *Rice*.

"And the bartender says, Why the long—" I urged them.

"Face!" Predictable Jack Spoar.

"Nope," I said. "Not that old chestnut. Try again."

"Penis!"

"C'mon. Use your imaginations."

"Erection! I know it's erection!"

"Is that funny? Do you think that's really funny?"

"Well . ."

"Okay. Now," I said. "Visualize. What's funny—what's *odd* about the Buddha?"

"Teeth?" Molly O'Healey offered cautiously. "My what big teeth you have?"

"Molly," I sighed pedantically. "This is not Little Red Riding Hood."

"That's right," Mr. Kang agreed. "The Buddha doesn't have teeth. Not even in Pyongyang."

"Eyelashes," Ms Grabor-Hepinstall interposed confidently and flashed hers.

"Well," I said. "You're getting warmer. Now—"

All of a sudden there was a sort of whooshing sound and the Alien appeared in the doorway. I was certain I had closed it.

"Jesus Christ," it hissed. "For Christ's sake, earlobes. The Buddha walks into this bar and the bartender says, Why the long *earlobes*?"

"Justine!" Ms Grabor-Hepinstall cried and grinned conspiratorially.

"Justine!" the rest of the group erupted gleefully.

"Is that you?"

"Are you back?"

"Where ya been?"

"You're not dead after all!"

"Happy Halloween!"

And just as suddenly the Alien was gone. Just like that. I went to the door and looked down the hallway and glimpsed a shape disappear into the stairwell. I do not know why they called it Justine. Perhaps there was some kind of tell operating just below the level of awareness. And I knew Justine and Ms Grabor-Hepinstall had been thick as thieves when the occasion called for it back in the day. As I turned back to the class it dawned on me that they just might be messing with me. They liked to mess with me and I liked them to mess with me. I encouraged it. Comedy is all about getting under the other guy's skin. That is why we call it needling. Maybe that is why women are so good at it in their way—they are so uncommonly precise with needles. Justine almost surgical—and no anesthetic. At any rate it comes natural to humans—like dancing and murder and betrayal and nervous breakdowns. We went through a few more exercises and at last I wrapped things up. By the end of the hour they were all starting to look a little bit like Aliens to me now. Aliens with needles.

"That Hazmat suit thing," I asked Jack Spoar as he was going out the door. "Why did you call it Justine?"

"I don't know," he said. "I was just following the others."

*

In his office McPheeters wore a Tartan kilt with a furry sporran that sat on his lap like a lewd pet and a sort of mountain green Bavarian hunting blazer with leather lapels. His businesslike blue socks were held up by garters strapped around his thick bare calves. His necktie was equally blue and businesslike. A pair of iron gray house slippers rounded out the ensemble. There are people who can wear motley like a uniform and he was one of them.

We stared at each other in silence across his coffee table. He sat high in his big armchair and I sat low on the legless sofa. His days as a shyster were evident even in the relative heights and displacement of the furniture in his office. He operated the Long Pig for its income stream but his real love was as the island's only licensed ambulance chaser and debt collector. His office was his law office. He sipped once at his tumbler of Macallan neat and I sipped once at mine. McPheeters winced.

"Last night," McPheeters said.

"Like I said over the phone. Thought maybe it was from Public Health. Or the Insiders leaning on you a little. A raid or whatever. Thought I'd give you a heads up."

"Appears somebody you know hit the jackpot."

"Huh?" I said.

"That Hazmat suit that picked up an order of ribs for you. Asked if you still liked the bourbon glaze."

"Some joker pretending to be Justine. Maybe somebody the kids put up to it. Gretchen or Veronique maybe. Those babes would do just about anything for a few laughs and a handful of escuchos. Or even Yumi—taking a little revenge. She knew a lot of our secrets. Can't figure out how they managed the blimp though. Swear I saw one out there over the parking lot in the dark last night. Anyhow Halloween's just around the corner. Had me going for a while."

"Getting an Upgrade."

"Upgrade. What's an Upgrade?"

"You haven't read the *Gnome and the Genome*?"

"Don't read much science these days. Makes me feel antiquated. Don't need any more of that."

"More's the pity. By that Greek chap. Won a Nobel. For that and their work on marine tectonics. Quite the Renaissance man. At the Max Planck now."

"Max Plank," I said. "Who's he—some sort of porn film star?"

"Ever the comedian, Harold. Ever the comedian."

McPheeters leaned over and combed his bookshelf.

"Thought I had it here," he said. "Must be at home."

"What's an Upgrade?"

"Kind of like cosmetic surgery. Without the scalpels and hammers, as I understand. Or the rack without the dislocation of joints. As I understand. Turns you into a sort of half breed Insider, I guess you could say. Sets one back a small fortune, I hear."

"That's an Upgrade?"

"They tweak the brain a little too. Just enough to get them into Mensa."

"I don't believe any of this shit, Angus."

"They call it Evol Hum. The Hazmat suit is just a big bandage. Like a cocoon."

"You're nuts."

"Suit yourself. It's in the book."

"I know a joke when I see one."

"Do you," McPheeters said. "Do you really?"

McPheeters stood up with ponderous slowness. There was something of the centaur or even Houyhnhnm about him in his three hundred pound frame—and you felt his towering height ought to be measured in hands than in feet and inches. And his weight in stone. He walked over to the little sink and dumped the contents of his tumbler into it.

"They call this shit whisky? It tastes like hair oil."

"Where'd you get it?"

"A client. Bogus black market drizzle. Thought maybe this one would not be so bad. Glad I brought the gun in today. He's coming in later this afternoon. Maybe take him out for a little target practice afterwards. Let him know not to fuck around."

"Nice bottle though. Macallan."

"Nice bottle." He took my tumbler and dumped it in the sink as well and sat down again. "They drill a hole in the bottom and draw out half the good stuff and fill it back up with rotgut. See," he shoved the bottom of the bottle in my face.

"Clever bastards," I said.

"Clever bastards," McPheeters said. "There are a hell of a lot of other ones around here too. But I groused about those Insider characters enough back in April when that poor big island gal and her unborn baby died inside those walls down at the far end of the beach. A bit too much of A Law Unto Themselves, I'm afraid."

"You're serious," I said. "They're that smart, those characters? They can really do Upgrades?"

IV.

A gondola was tied up near the footbridge. It was the same one I had seen drift by before. The same gondolier. He was awake now and we agreed on a fare and he pushed off and we glided quietly past the old Selkirk building where I work. We glided past the little abandoned automobile dealership with its big cracked show windows and a few rotting hulks in the parking lot out front. The wheels and tires on them were gone and the hoods and trunk lids were sprung. Still they looked at peace and could have been grazing out their last days if there had been anything else under them except concrete. We passed the shopping mall. Most of the shops were closed up but the Cannabis Emporium was still going full tilt. Thank god for that. Stoners were my bread and butter crowd at my occasional Saturday night gig at the Patio or the Orion. They couldn't follow a storyline more than a minute long but cracked up when a delayed pun exploded in their heads like a Zen revelation: *Sasquatches are rarely spotted in the Sierras—but when they are—they look like gorillas in leopard leotards.* We glided by some empty lots that were fenced off for no apparent reason. Maybe somebody wanted us to think they were going to build something there someday. There were a few squatters burning stuff in steel barrels but they did not look hard to move. The squatters, I mean. Up ahead in the distance I could make out the turrets and domes peeking over the high pink walls of the Casbah at the far end of the beach. We called it the Casbah. The Insiders who stayed

30

there did not call it that. Toby Pizzadazz came up with the name one drunken night on the beach at the Iguana Hutch and it stuck. The turrets and domes gleamed in the setting sun. I could smell the ocean now and the charcoal braziers up ahead. The gondolier turned to me.

"Where you want to get off?"

"Anywhere's okay. The Patio open yet?"

"Think so. Don't know about the Orion or the Iguana Hutch."

"Good," I said. Then: "Where you from?"

The gondolier stared at me and looked at the money in the palm of his hand as if it were some kind of bribe.

"Here and there."

"Mostly there, huh?" I said. I had not meant to be nosy.

"Mostly there, yes."

I debarked at the rusted Tsunami Evacuation Route sign for the tourists who no longer came. Its arrow pointed inland toward the high ground and the Blue Hole water hazard adjacent the old eighteenth fairway. Water hazard— nice touch, I thought, that.

The Pythoness sat on a high stool at the end of the Patio bar near the canal landing, her golden brown mismatched legs crossed and her brief skirt up past mid thigh. She smiled wanly as I took a seat at the bar next to the little stage where the band played. I did not want to get in her way. In the big glass bowl on the bar in front of her half a dozen tiny white lab mice sniffed curiously at the outside world or curled up and napped in blind contentment. For three hundred escuchos she would pluck one out and swallow it live in a single gulping pulse of her slender throat. When a mark caught her palming a mouse one night and slipping it into a pocket sewn into the inside of her skirt, everybody gathered around her protectively. We offered him his three hundred escuchos back if he would get up and leave and not come back. He smiled and shrugged and elected to stay. The three hundred escuchos was worth it, he said. The display of loyalty. One of her legs was shorter than the other and when she walked her pelvic cradle rocked sidewise like it was worked by a cam. No doubt there was not one among us that did not wonder what she looked like when she did that with no clothes on. Women can be Mysterious just by walking through your head. And the mouse swallowing business was not always an act. She just did not see the point of killing a fellow creature for chump change. After all, we're all mammals, the Pythoness explained. For a thousand escuchos the show was for real—that was our best guess anyhow—for takers were few and far between at this end of the beach.

Three workmen in thick boots and heavy duty waterproof workpants came in for drinks. Their faces were dark from the sun. They took a table with a big green umbrella. Their English was broken but they knew what to order. Hoppy brought them two small green bottles and three small glasses. The men poured for each other in turn but not for themselves. They were casual but there was something of a ritual about it too. Only after they had downed a glassful and poured another did they look around the patio. The one with authority ignored the Pythoness but fixed on her glass bowl. *Jwee*, he said. *Jwee*. When their grilled squid came on a big platter they ate greedily but squeamishly too. The three of them couldn't take their eyes off the mice. It was as if they thought the mice were watching them back. When the food was gone they got even more serious about the bottles and pouring glassfuls for each other and forgot about the mice.

"*Yep-poo-dah*! *Ah-eesh*!" the one in authority announced broadly, almost insolently. He had a white hard hat on and the other two wore yellow ones. I took it he was their foreman.

"*Joo-kee-duh-rah*!" he went on sharply and the three of them clinked glasses. "*Yo-jah-dul*! *Gut-nay-joo-yut-jee*! *Jaw-run gul bo-go-do il-ul ha-da-ni shin-tong-ha-goon*!"

I did not look at them straight on. I did not want them to think I was listening in. It was more fun that way. Sometimes you can even learn something too.

Years before on board the SS *Gale Storm* my gig was to set up sound equipment and work the light shows and accomplish other highly technical feats of stage engineering. Once or twice a week I subbed for the ship's standup comedian when he was too drunk or otherwise engaged flirting with the gray haired matronly passengers to do his dream job. (Dream job, yes: seniors don't heckle. Of course they don't laugh themselves to tears that much either.) That was why he got me the slot in the first place. But I was Crew, not Entertainment, and bunked with crew. I played cards belowdecks with the young Koreans from

Food Service and did not complain when they talked to each other in their own tongue. In fact they were all college kids studying Tourism Management or something like that. They were learning the business from the waterline up, so to speak. The job was part of their education and to make the most of their time on board they begged me to correct their English. They were big on correctness. They offered to teach me their language in exchange. I told them the only thing I wanted to learn a language for was to get laid and stay out of the cooler. I meant it as a joke and they thought it was great fun since there were not any Korean women around to get offended. That's how I could untangle what the workmen were talking about. Basic Yahoo Korean: *Beautiful! Jesus Fuck! It was killing me! What women! It was unbelievable! It's a wonder how you guys get any work done!*

My chicken breast arrived. It was cross-hatched nicely on both sides by the charcoal brazier in the open air kitchen. I do not care what they say about animal rights and the new chickens that can play chess if you give them a keyboard with the right pictures on it—with peas and mashed potatoes you cannot beat the Patio's chicken. And would it be so bad to end up on a brazier at the end of your brief journey? Take a walk through a graveyard some afternoon after a heavy rain and think about what's under your feet.

V.

I hitched a ride with the three workmen. They drove an electric dune buggy with balloon tires that rode easily over the sand and seats you could fold up or down. They worked on the big sand dredger, they said.

"It is hard work in this heat." One of the yellow hats spoke tolerable English so I did not have to embarrass myself with my Yahoo Korean.

The beach was still being built up down at the far end though you could not see what they were doing behind the big walls of the Casbah that extended down into the water. But you could see the dredger four or five hundred yards out sucking up sand from the bottom of the bay. The workmen bunked out on the dredger and breakfasted there so they could be up and at it at dawn. They occasionally ate dinner on the beach or just went for drinks at the Patio or the Orion but they were not supposed to mingle with the locals. That was discouraged. They were not supposed to talk about what they saw. I asked them if this meant the women. I did not mean to be nosy but they clammed up. Big deal, I thought. A nude beach from five hundred yards out. Who cares? But maybe it was a big deal to them out on a dredger all night with nobody but each other for company.

We passed what was left of the Holiday Sands and La Concha and the Majestic. The Holiday Sands had gone under first. It looked a little ghostly in the moonlight but in the daylight it was just a lot of busted up cinderblocks and stucco facing and plumbing that went nowhere. La Concha and the Majestic likewise. It could have been a typhoon or even a tsunami that had leveled them but the Crash had done the job nicely. It just took a little longer and a little help from looters. When La Concha closed its doors we had a gay old time polishing off the last of the booze behind the Roaring Twenties Lounge zinc bar. Joker Fernandez was a sport about that. Fuck it, he said. To Wall Street, Angry Stan raised a glass and toasted bitterly and the rest of us chimed in about who expected to pull up stakes and move on and who was planning to stick around. Well the rest of them did, anyhow. They were young and just starting out and their eyes dazzled at the prospect of change. The standup and music gig venues of the Holiday Sands and the Majestic and La Concha were a chapter and a memory to be cherished. I caught Stan's eyes across the room and we nodded solemnly. Sure, he was not the old timer I was, but had set down roots too.

The beach was some three miles long and the workmen were in no hurry to get back to their dredger. We stopped once and the foreman broke open a little green bottle of the hooch they had been drinking back at the Patio. Glasses were passed around. These guys did not pass a bottle around. Perhaps they did not savor human backwash. But we ended up sharing glasses anyways because there were only three of them and four of us.

The foreman said something in Korean. I understood but the yellow hard hat who spoke English translated for me before I had a chance to answer: How old are you?

When you drink with Koreans the first thing you have

to establish is everybody's age. They are hierarchical to the backbone. They cannot relax until they know who is the oldest. I learned this from the kids on the *Storm*. You may not exchange names—but you always exchange ages. Even a single year of seniority gave you all sorts of bragging rights and privileges.

"Forty eight," I said, knocking off a couple of years I spent doing nothing in a place I did not like to talk about with a cellmate nick-named The Claw Hammer. How was I to know Keith was packing ten kilos under the floorboard of his van. Or that the heat was onto him.

The foreman relaxed. He was older and this gave him a little rush of satisfaction. You could see it in his eyes.

"I am fifty two," he said and we toasted order and rank and harmony.

We finished off the bottle and got back underway. At the check point a night guard signaled for us to halt. He raised his arm and we saw the flat of his hand. There were two other guards in a corrugated metal rain shelter behind him. They all wore purple fez caps with brown faces underneath. Their jowls were deeply lined and were not clean shaven. They looked like they had been recruited from some obscure foreign legion. They made me think of distant empires that had gone belly up but long ago. I had seen purple fez caps and brown faces in town going in and out of Aye, Claudia's. They were not stuck out on a dredger all night. The two guards under the shelter ignored us and went on playing cards. The foreman said something and jerked his thumb at me in the backseat. I did not catch what he said. The guard splashed his flashlight in my face and I stared down at the floorboards of the buggy. Damn it I thought and started to get out to walk back. Suddenly the buggy jerked forward and I fell back in my seat and we eased past the check point. I looked back and saw the guard standing there with a green bottle in his hand.

Up near where the wall began we stopped and we all got out. A small pontoon water taxi sat in the water. If you did not know it was there you would never have seen it. The three workmen got in. I heard the clink of full bottles in a canvas sack the yellow hard hat who spoke some English was carrying. He was the youngest of the group and did the dirty work. At any rate they were well provisioned for the night. They pushed off and the foreman called out to me. He spoke a little more English than "I am fifty two" after all. I should have known.

"You go to wall. You look around five minutes okay. Then you go back. Then you scram. Then you beat it."

When the workmen were out of sight, I stripped down and waded into the surf. Once I was in waist deep I got ready to slip into a shallow dive. But the water was too dark, too black. I wanted to get out past where the wall ended and see if I could get a look at the beach. But I did not intend to die trying. I went in chest deep and pulled myself along the wall, touching the sandy bottom with my feet and keeping an eye on the top of the wall where guards might be. With each foot of extended beach the island was growing. I wanted to see that. In a thousand years perhaps it would reach across the strait and touch the big island again.

It was then a spotlight hit me from overhead. Its glare bore down on me with such ferocity my ears shouted. I heard voices behind it, muffled at first and then clearer.

"Beat it!" one hissed. It was a familiar hiss.

"Oh don't scare it," a second voice boomed and sang, sweet and at the same time thunderous. It was no Alien hiss. "It's so cute!"

"Look at its little hands! They're just like ours! Can you see its penis?"

"No, it's under the water."

"I want to see its penis!"

"Out!" the first voice hissed. The spotlight moved back to the beach like it was pointing the way. Three figures stood on top of the wall. I could see them now with the spotlight out of my eyes. An Alien and two women. The women were tall. Tall by anyone's standard. And nude. Not naked—but nude the way statues in a museum are nude. In the blue lamps along the top of the wall their torsos and breasts glowed a bluish gray.

"Does it have an erection? I want to see its erection."

I was out of the water now and scrambling for my clothes.

"I see it now. Do you see it? Do you see its cute little erection? I bet it's not but six inches long."

My body had obliged them.

I could not tell the voices apart. The women sounded just the same. They were thrilling voices in the stillness of the night but at the same time I hated them. I could not but obey them.

"I want to see it jerk off. I like to watch them jerk off. It's so disgusting."

My hand began to oblige. Really I could not hold back. I do not know why. The spotlight was on me now and I was clothed in light. Frozen in it. When I finished there was a little dark spot on the sand at my feet.

"Huh," a voice said. "Huh."

"What a cute little old—old—old *man*." The *man* came to her only reluctantly. Her voice sounded puzzled that it was the best she could do.

VI.

In the morning I went to brush my teeth but there was no toothpaste in the tube. There was only a smidgen of it left in the neck of the tube where you screw the cap on. Worse, there was no backup in the closet off the kitchen. I am usually careful about that. But there was none. Not this time. Just a couple of dusty old bottles of Justine's Quixotone lotion. I squeezed the shoulder of the toothpaste tube to force the last smidgen out of the neck. I used both hands. But when I got this last smidgen out, I had to let go one hand in order to bring the toothbrush up to the mouth of the tube. And when I did this the little bit of toothpaste scooted back into the neck of the tube like a tiny fearful creature pulling its head back inside its shell. I did this three times and the fourth time I finally got enough on the bristles of the toothbrush to brush my teeth.

I thought about this later as I sat on the toilet. How when you are at the doctor's office and you have to produce a stool sample and nothing will come out. Then a little comes out but you can't do a damned thing with it because it won't drop. This amused me mightily as I sat there. Was it Martin Luther who came up with his profoundest notions as he sat astride the crapper? Regardless, perhaps Jack Spoar could use it in his routine. He was fearless at bathroom humor but in the analogy imagination department he was no great shakes. I wrote down what I just said here about the toothpaste and the stool sample and decided to pass it along. The Open Mike Nite field trip was coming up and

I wanted him to be ready. And I wanted Molly to see Jack bring down the house—or at least not flop. She was the kid sister of the group and had not yet gone up. I wanted him to have a good night and I wanted her to want to have a night like his. I wanted her to see how easy it was.

A shower and a deep towel off and half a carafe of rich drip set me up for the rest of the morning. Something scrabbled in the kitchen ceiling overhead. Perhaps the iguanas had gotten into the crawl space again. If they were not careful a couple of them just might end up in a pot one of these days. Maybe I would invite the Pythoness over. Or Miss Soobiah back at my office. Hoppy had a recipe he swore by. He would show me how to make the Achiote oil. Good for my gouty big toe too, he guaranteed. It had been quiet for months but my long walk back from the beach had jaked it into an ugly splay.

I went into the bathroom for a leak and when I came out the Alien was sitting on the sofa and the overhead light was turned off and the shades were drawn. The front of its headpiece was swung open to the side. The face of Justine stared out. Well, it was Justine's face and it wasn't. I honestly could not make up my mind. It was masked in a filmy veil like a spider might have spun and spun over it. No, it was Justine all right. Her brow, her nose and cheekbones, her chin. Her lips and eyes. But inside the headpiece she looked like a ghostly nun in a wimple—a Sister of Charity from some far off galaxy. Frowning.

"I didn't hear the water running."

Not again, I thought. Not again. How many times had we been through this routine.

"You didn't wash your hands."

We were picking up right where we left off. How many times, oh Lord.

"How can you hear anything in that damned suit anyhow?" I said. "Take it off."

"I can't. My boobs aren't ready yet. Neither is the rest of me."

"I don't know what you are talking about," I said. "And anyhow, you're supposed to be dead. Old Santana found your clothes on the beach that night. Everybody figured—"

"I guess I just wanted to keep you guessing."

"You put me through hell."

"I put you through hell? *You* put *me* through hell."

Good Christ, I thought. What is this—a fucking echo chamber.

"Well, at least you are not hissing now. But the carry out pork ribs was a nice touch. You really had me going."

"Thanks. Piece of meat."

"Piece of meat," I agreed. "And the airship. That was a nice touch too."

"Got friends."

"Okay, now, really. Where you been for five fucking months?"

"I'm being Upgraded," the face of Justine said flatly. She flicked her tongue at a corner of her mouth to whisk away a stray filament of veil.

"You're shitting me!"

"I am."

"What did you do? Sell your soul to some Space Cowboy Mephistopheles? McPheeters said it cost an arm—"

"I got lucky."

"Lucky?" I said

"I had to go, Harold. It was my big chance. And you didn't want me anymore."

"That's not so and you know it. We talked about that."

"A rich Greek took a liking to me. He likes my stuff. Loves a good laugh. Says I have class. Wants to make me into an Insider Companion. Is making me into an Insider Companion. That's why I'm in this damned suit. This damned cocoon. Getting a new body lift."

"Where is he now?"

"He's coming tomorrow. Told him I wanted to come ahead. See some old friends. See you."

"Well," I said. "You've seen me. What now?"

"Oh Harold. Can't we start over?"

"Darling," I cried. I bent over to kiss her but her lips were too far inside the headpiece of the Hazmat suit. I could not get my own lips in there. And the filmy veil put me off a little too. She looked like she belonged in one of those *Leper Bride from Pluto* movies. And we were laughing so hard by now we could not have kissed anyway. "Sure," I said. "Let's start over."

"I didn't hear the water running," the face of Justine began. *"You didn't wash your hands."*

"Urine is sterile."

"Urine?"

"Piss, then."

"Urine is such an ugly word. Piss is better. Pee is even better than that."

"I agree. Did you know the Romans brushed their teeth with the stuff? To whiten them. It's in Catullus."

"I know. Ammonia. Like bleach."

"Right. They especially prized Spanish piss. It got even stronger on the long journey to Rome."

"Tell me something, Harold."

"What's that?"

"Can I ask you a question?"

"Go ahead."

"It's a little—I don't know—"

"Try me."

"Well, did you ever pee in a woman's mouth?"

"What a question!"

"Well?"

"Sure. Once."

"Really? You really did?"

"Once. Like I said."

"Did you pay her or something?"

"She came into the bathroom. Knelt down beside me while I was about to take a wizz."

"How did you know what she wanted?"

"She just sort of sat there on her knees."

"Looking up into your eyes like a puppy? Or staring at your dick?"

"I don't remember. It was a long time ago."

"But you knew what she wanted."

"It was strange. She didn't say anything. I didn't either."

"But you knew what she wanted? Like telepathy?"

"I did."

"And?"

"It was the closest I've ever felt to being back inside the womb."

"More like peeing in a swimming pool, I'd say. Like a kid."

"It was a kind of quiet ecstasy. No struggle. Just an easy release. I could have been asleep."

"What was her name?"

"I don't remember now."

"But you remember pissing in her mouth. You remember that."

"It's the one thing about her I never forgot."

"You said it's sterile. Urine's really sterile?"

"That's what the books say."

"And she swallowed it—all of it?"

"She emptied me."

"But you don't remember her name?"

"I don't."

"That's disgusting. That's the part that's so disgusting."

"I'm sorry."

"That's okay. I just hate it when men don't remember what we do for them."

"Give Piss a Chance. God," I said. "I love that routine."

"You're a genius, Harold. It was the last one we did together. Remember?"

"They booed us off the stage at the Twenties. Fucking Shriners and their wives from Rhode Island."

"An artist. Nobody appreciates—"

"Let's go into the bathroom together. Now."

"Don't be ridiculous."

"It would inspire me. I am sure of it."

"Don't hand me that bullshit."

"Then show me your tits at least."

"I can't. This Hazmat suit. I told you that."

"They always inspired me. Remember that riff I—"

"That was then. I am spoken for now."

"Spoken for. How quaint."

"You never should have dropped me from the act."

"It was for your own good. You were ready to go out on your own."

"Whatever," the face of Justine said with a weary finality.

"Okay," I said. "Okay. I get it. Let's not fight."

"We're not fighting."

"Anyhow—what's with the filmy veil stuff. You look like you just crept out of a crypt or something."

"Protection. I'm not supposed to expose myself to the light just yet. Bad for my complexion. I even have to go to the bathroom in the dark. I'm taking a big risk right now."

"Sun block for Insider Aliens."

"Something like that."

"So what's that stuff taste like?"

"Cotton candy," the face of Justine said. "But sort of salty."

Justine stood up from the sofa. She looked around the room.

"I just wanted you to know. That I'll be okay. That's all. Before you left. As if you cared."

"I'm not leaving. This is my home too. And you know that."

"Harold," the face of Justine said. "Do your bloody promises mean nothing?"

"Promise? What promise?"

"You know bloody well. The night before last I brought you the ribs from the Long Pig."

"That wasn't made in good faith. I didn't know it was really you. You were fucking with my head."

"You promised!"

"Well I'm not leaving. Sorry."

"Harold, you are just like that damned autistic *I prefer not to* guy we read about in college."

"Shut your damned—visor, Justine," I said. "Before I shut it for you."

"That's not my name anymore."

"Whatever," I said, and wondered if this too was part of some routine but only dimly remembered.

VII.

"No! Mr. Kang!" I shouted and leaped from my chair. "No!"

Mr. Kang stood by the bar and the Pythoness's glass bowl. His hand was inside the bowl. There was a three hundred escucho note on the bar next to the bowl.

"What in the world are you doing, Mr. Kang?"

I had him by the arm now. The arm that was inside the bowl and the hand that was cradling a white mouse.

"You can't do that!"

Mr. Kang stared at me stupidly. Perplexed. Our eyes locked.

Everyone at the table was looking at us.

"They are not for customers," I said. I would not let go his arm until he let go the mouse. "They are not snacks."

Mr. Kang gaped searchingly at his classmates at the table. Jack Spoar was laughing.

"He doesn't want to eat it," Molly said. "He's lonely."

"He wants a pet," Ms Grabor-Hepinstall said.

"Huh?"

"He said he wants a pet."

"I have never seen a white mouse before. They are beautiful. So rice white."

"Still," I said. "You better let it go."

He let the mouse go. It seemed unfazed. It clambered at the side of the bowl on its back legs and sniffed at Mr. Kang through the glass.

"Sorry," I said. "They belong to the Pythoness. They're the Pythoness's."

There were some embarrassed titters but Jack Spoar was howling.

I sat down again.

"Sorry."

Mr. Kang sat down too. His three hundred escucho note stayed on the bar next to the sign that said 300 ESCUCHOS. He was not giving up.

"Three hundred escuchos is a lot to pay for a mouse," I explained. I wanted to change the subject.

"Good grief," Ms Grabor-Hepinstall said. She did not want to change the subject. To see a teacher humbled is a special treat for some students.

"Okay," I said. "If the Pythoness wants to sell you one, okay. It's none of our business. And you can do whatever you want with it."

Mr. Kang had arrived at the Patio dressed as a dude ranch cowboy. I do not know why. Maybe he liked the extra height the boots gave him, but the sheriff's badge and spurs were a bit over the top. That is why I had panicked. I thought maybe he was going to show off some more. Then again, Halloween was just around the corner.

The Pythoness hobbled back in from the ladies room and Mr. Kang was out of his chair again. He cupped her elbow in the palm of his hand and spoke to her meaningfully. With his other hand he pointed at the mice in the bowl. The Pythoness ignored him and scoured the room for takers. Open Mike Nite was not good for business until people got a little oiled and the jokes began to repeat themselves.

Angry Stan was the MC for the evening. Tall and fit he spoke with a sly and disarming gravelly barroom drawl and took in the crowd with the cool wariness of a counter puncher—and if you saw a hint of fear in his eyes it was fear for *your* life, not *his*. This got your attention and did not let it go. It made no difference whether you were from Zanzibar or the Aleutians. On stage he was a boxer as much as a comic. He jabbed at you with his eyes and you ducked with a grin that was not far from a grimace. Still you laughed and when he wound up his routine you wanted him to come out of his corner and go another round. But the blood on canvas was his, not yours. He once told me if he tried to do standup for a living he would wind up in the bughouse. No one I know ever saw any reason to doubt him.

In the audience we had the usual crowd. A healthy handful of locals, maybe half a dozen of whom would step up on stage when their turns came. A scattering of sunbaked backpacker couples with cameras and expensive lenses and freshly washed doo rags on their heads. The women's thighs were lean and fit and tan and you envied their partners. The Mormon missionaries never showed up but the World Church of the Word codger and his Balinese boytoy sat at a little table in the corner. The three workmen from the sand dredger dropped in. Their workaday yellow and white beetle hard hats offered a nice contrast to the happy go lucky indigo and mauve butterfly doo rags. They did not seem to know about the show and looked a little out of their depth as they found a table and ordered their dried squid snacks and little green bottles. I sat with my own group at a table near the stage. It was best to get them comfortable in front of the audience they were going to face. And it made it harder to chicken out. There were five of us: Mr. Kang, Jack Spoar, Ms Grabor-Hepinstall, Molly and myself. Molly was not going to perform. She was the latest to move up from Intermediate to Advanced and felt she was not "ready"—as if anybody really ever is. Layla "Iguana Donna" Hallicks-Jukes was back at Duke defending her dissertation on Great Toe Abduction Among Our Pliocene Pongid Ancestors, which was not—she ever hastened to point out—about prehistoric kidnapping practices, and Skip Townes was in rehab again on the big island.

A tall Insider couple filed into the back of the Patio at the last minute and drew stares. They certainly did not fit in. They were gorgeous, as people used to say. And tall as Christmas trees in a family living room where you have to stand on a little step stool to set the star on top. The woman might have been one of the giantesses on top of the wall from the other night, I could not be sure. For all her height she moved like she was to the ballroom born, supple and poised in a short tunic. In her high heel boots she carried her butt so high off the floor that you thought you could almost dance with it cheek to cheek. But touching her would be like trying to use rubber gloves as an oven mitt. Your skin, you thought, would melt. Or freeze. And with them an Alien in a black and orange Hazmat suit in tow. I should have expected that. And a nice complement to Mr. Kang in his dude ranch getup as he stood at the bar and chatted up the Pythoness and her bowl of white mice.

Angry Stan took the microphone from the clip of the mike stand and blew into it. It worked fine. "Okay," he announced. "Welcome to the Patio Open Mike Nite for October. Tonight—"

"SLUT! FREAK!"

All the heads in the audience whirled and faced the back of the patio. The Pythoness had lunged at the Alien and was scrabbling viciously at the little rectangular window on the front of its headpiece. The Alien had the Pythoness gripped by the wrists and together their hands and arms moved sideways this way and that almost like they were dancing.

"TAKE THAT THING OFF!"

Mr. Kang had the Pythoness around the middle now but could barely keep a grip. She had no hips—she was all waist. Finally he got kind of a Heimlich maneuver hold on her but before he could pull her off the Alien the front of its headpiece popped open and swung to the side.

It was not Justine. Or maybe it was. In the darkness I was too far way to see. But whatever was in the Hazmat suit squealed like a stuck pig.

"MY FACE! OH MY GOD MY FACE!"

The Alien jumped up and shoved the Pythoness into Mr. Kang's arms and fled into the ladies room. The Insider female followed her in. When the Pythoness made to pursue them the male Insider seized her by the throat just under her jaw and lifted her up so that her short leg dangled in the air and the toe of the foot of her good leg dibbled at the floor. He said something to her you could not hear and she went limp and then he sat her down on her barstool. It was all over in a minute.

"Ladies and gentlemen." People were looking to Angry Stan for explanation. For guidance. "A big hand for our friends from Halloween Land down the beach. They'll be passing out complimentary blimp passes for the Blue Hole Tour at the end of the show." The male Insider gave Stan a stern, savage look. "Now let's get this madness out of our systems before they lock us all UP!"

VIII.

Toby Pizzadazz kicked off the evening. He was the only male in the room shorter than myself and his khaki safari shorts reached down past mid calf. With his short arms and compact build you half expected him to launch himself into a handspring or two across the stage. He told a few tiny dick jokes and one about vomiting into a woman's cleavage as he danced with her and a fine one about how he really was not all that short—he was just standing farther away from us than we thought. But the audience was too busy wiping the barf off the joke woman's boobs to appreciate it. This provoked an imp of inspiration and I took out my script and jotted down a few quick notes on the back: *Intel joke—In college dated Phil major—Called me her Lil Tommy Hobbes—Said because I was so Nasty, Brutish & Short.* Toby was followed by Irishman Lorcan Teague who rattled off half a dozen Drunks in a Graveyard jokes. They were fun but a few minutes later you could not remember any of them to write them down. As a lapsed Catholic he felt obliged to tell a story about a lecherous priest and a pug ugly nun trapped in the rectory during a blackout and this drew a few scattered titters. I prayed there would not be too many more genitalia jokes—it might spoil my own routine when my slot rolled around at the end of the evening.

Next up our own Ms Grabor-Hepinstall, ever the bored sophisticate in class, led off with a playful send up of psychoanalysis. *Freud,* she began, *divided the human personality up into three parts: the Id, the Ego, and the Super*

Lumbago. Droll, but she was flirting with trouble if she went esoteric on the crowd. Wisely she performed a neat pirouette to the Putative Discoverer of the Americas and another amusing triplet. *Columbus set out for the New World on three ships: the Niña, the Pinta, and the Diarrhea.* Great fun, again, but when she got to *The Three Monastic Vows: Poverty, Chastity and Obesity* I was tapping my foot and thirsting for a second beer. Good for you, still, Vivienne— ride that old one trick pony of your own into the sunset.

The patio filled with a hush and a few murmurs as she finished up. The Alien and the Insider female had come back in from the ladies' room and taken their seats. Everyone pretended that nothing had happened. I did not want to look around but could not help myself. The Insider female sat expressionless and her male escort whispered something in her ear. The little window of the Alien's headpiece was back in place. What in the hell were they doing here in the first place, I wondered indignantly. Slumming? Bitches. Didn't they have their own fine entertainment in their Casbah down at the far end of the beach. White people, I thought perversely. No wonder Black people always hated us so.

Ruth Beth and Drago Voinovich showed a short film about children. Drago pronounced it "filim". We had all forgotten how priceless kids could be just being kids. There had been only five left on the island when they filmed them. Now even those five were long gone. One boy fell down and started to cry and everyone in the audience teared up. Then people started to get nervous—you could sense a stillness in the crowd, a holding of breath. Maybe they were feeling a little guilty about agreeing not to keep any children on the island anymore. The Insiders were uncomfortable with kids and did not want them around. Maybe they did not want kids around if things got nasty. Maybe they were a little more human than we gave them credit for. Still that was hard to square with the rumors about the dead big island gal and her unborn baby. Go figure. At any rate, those were the first families—the ones with kids—to be given offers to leave. The most generous offers, it turned out. Orders, really. Offers they could not refuse. The five kids in the film were the last of the kids. Everyone had agreed to the whole business. Nobody blamed anybody else. But in a way it was like some dark fairy tale come true. Still the film was funny. The kids were cute and got a big round of tickled if weepy applause.

Mr. Kang cracked us all up with his endearingly screwball English. *When I first arrived here from North Korea, I was still a little green behind the ears.* You could not help but crane around to try to get a look at the sides of his head. *I guess up here in this cowboy outfit I must stick out like a green thumb.* What is it with this green stuff, I wondered, but at least he was off rice—for a while. *Back in North Korea if you wanted to survive you had better know where all the dirty laundry is buried.* There was a crazy kind of poetry here. You saw people furtively digging holes in their backyards in the moonlight and a big washbasket of soiled underwear. *We didn't have Love Hotels there like you have here. In North Korea we had Hate Hotels. You lied in bed in the darkness with your partner and whispered, "I hated your guts the first time I ever laid eyes on you. I never thought I could hate you more than I hated you at that moment, but I do."* He told a cannibalism joke about a military plane crash and a lot of dead soldiers lying around in uniforms and a host of villagers coming upon the scene and rubbing their hands together in anticipation and going *Ooh ooh. Government rice. No barley mixed in. Ooh ooh. Government rice.* Mr. Kang was getting downright scary now and I was glad he kept it well under his six minutes. Up on stage he never took his eyes off the Pythoness and her glass bowl of white mice and you had to wonder what was going on in her head too.

Jack Spoar's turn came up next but he was nowhere to be found in the crowd. We all looked around. No Jack. This miffed me. Cold feet, perhaps, but nobody was more uninhibited than he was. He had my toothpaste–stool sample prompt too. It was sure fire, I was certain. I got up and walked to the back of the patio and stuck my head in the men's room. No Jack. Had the Insider couple and their Alien sidekick spooked him? Not likely. Still, he was nowhere. MIA. I had wanted him to be good so I could be better. In stand up you can feed off each other. You prime the audience for the next clown. We are like that. It is a thing you learn early—almost by instinct. Competition and cooperation go hand in glove. Fist. I wanted to punch him.

And if it really was Justine inside that Alien costume tonight, I wanted her to remember all the laughs we had had together. To relive them. I shelved my Sex Organ Donor Card routine for the evening and from the recesses of memory dusted off the monologue about the museums and cafes and eateries and street mimes of Europe the year before. The one we scripted together when we got back, raunchy and offensive as it might be to the squeaky clean backpackers in their colorful doo rags in the audience. But I wanted to see that damned black and orange Hazmat suit split its sides. That little window on its headpiece to look up at me and mirror–

"—everybody's favorite comedy teacher," Angry Stan announced, "will lesson us again in the art of stand up—Harry—the Rat Catcher in the Wry—Ratner!"

We were visiting Vienna a while back, I began kind of in the middle of things. Jack's non appearance had thrown me off my game. My intro was gone—forgotten. I could not remember it. I had not knocked enough dust off it. But soldier on I had to up there on stage.

My ex-girlfriend and me. We were visiting Vienna where they don't call them art museums. They call them KUNST museums.

I pronounced *kunst* distastefully the way those cynical, darksided comics do *love* or *peace* or *kumbaya.*

That's right. Vienna is in Austria which is where Hitler was born. So they speak German there. Also they don't call it Vienna. They call it Wien. And they call the people there Wieners. Yep, wieners and kunst. You can't beat that combination. We went to a Kunst Museum to see the Dekadenz exhibit. There were a lot of naked women in the paintings on the walls. Yep, they really do spell it that way. Kunst. Don't ask me why. At the Kunst Museum a professor was lecturing to her students in German and pointing at a Klimt. I don't know why they spell it that way either.

This was not going well. It was sailing over people's heads. Without the introduction it was striking the wrong note. But it was too late to change horses. We were in Europe and we were stuck there.

Yeah, that's Art, I said. We like Art. But what I really like is Literature. A good book. I like to settle in with a good book. But you know the greatest monument of modern literature isn't in English at all. It isn't. It's in French and is called A La Reserche du Temps Perdu by a guy named Marcel Proust. Remembrance of Times Past is how it is sometimes translated. It's about seven volumes long. Seven books. It's about this guy named Marcel who takes a bite of a cookie one winter day at tea with his Aunt and suddenly his mind is flooded with memories of his childhood and past lovers and rivals and betrayals and so forth and this goes on for about seven books, like I said. Nobody's ever read it all through, of course. That's what greatness is all about. A monument, like I said.

The crowd could not see where this was going. I did not blame them. I had to get to the punch line but it seemed a long way off—like a dog paddler watching a ship growing ever smaller on the horizon.

Anyhow my ex and I were in Europe a while back and we stopped in Paris, France, on the last leg of our trip. We were watching our pennies by this time but one night we wanted to go out and eat a really good meal.

We went to a quaint little place abutting Notre Dame and I really wanted a steak. A beefsteak. You know how it is. A T-bone even—maybe it was the Flying Buttresses, I don't know. So we looked at the menu but the only steak we could really afford was something called steak tartare. So we ordered that.

Do you know what steak tartare actually is? It's a big patty of highly seasoned RAW ground beef. Raw ground beef as in UNCOOKED hamburger. I didn't know that. Not at all. So the waiter served it and I looked at it and I thought what the hell. I'm hungry.

I took one bite of this RAW GROUND BEEF and suddenly my mind was flooded with memories of all the PUSSY I had ever eaten in my life. It was shocking. But kind of a revelation too. Soon I found myself cutting my raw steak tartare into little meat triangles and then eating them and remembering like a madman. Like the Marcel guy with HIS cookie and HIS memories. I ate Sal's pussy and Lynn's vagina all over again and what's her name's quim who came to my 30th birthday party drunk as a skunk and her gash smelling like one too. Yeah, that same rancid stench that triggers a gravid cockroach to release its cache of eggs. I snacked again on Janine's snatch like the afternoon after she got off work at the hospital—and, oh yeah, one question: Can anyone here tell me why nurse pussy always tastes like disinfected hallways?

And then there was Monique and her little sister Marilyn. Catholic pussy. Ptah. Guys, you do not want to touch that. Maybe it's the odor of sanctity, I don't know. But they always tasted like a priest got there before me. Sort of an incense taste. Yeah—incense mixed with herring brine. Little Sisters of the Holy Mackerel Snapper, I called them. And anyhow inside they were as big as Notre Dame goddam cathedral, flying buttockses and all.

Anyhow, where was I? Oh yeah, I was cutting my steak tartare into these little meat triangles. And all the time Justine was sitting opposite me. And you know what she was doing? She was cutting up HER steak tartare into little meat dicks and forking them into her mouth like there was no tomorrow.

IX.

We adjourned to the Orion, Ms Grabor-Hepinstall giddy with the afterglow of success, Molly in her footsteps equally exuberant and confident she would step up to the mike the next time she got a chance. Mr. Kang would not leave the Patio without the Pythoness and the Pythoness would not leave without her glass bowl of mice. Hunched over her tote bag she could have been some ancient hominid whose ancestors had never quite achieved full erectness.

It was painful just to watch her walk that way. There had been a rumor the Pythoness first arrived on the island in the same Hazmat getup we spotted around now and again down at the far end of the beach. Trapped inside it, almost, or so Stan swore she complained cryptically to his wife one afternoon a couple months later when supposedly she was rid of the outfit. Perhaps it was true, though it made no sense at the time. Personally I thought she was a bit off her rail— like tonight back at the Patio. But Hoppy liked her around. He felt she lent his place a dash of off beat charm. And then again women in this part of the world have their secrets. At any rate, she had not hobbled back then. Nobody had ever seen a dippity Alien. Then sometime in early summer she took her place at the bar in the Patio with her glass bowl and gimped leg and the sign that read 300 ESCUCHOS. The Hazmat suit was gone, if she had ever really been in one. Just around the time Justine disappeared, oddly enough. This was about as much as anyone knew. That and her jaked leg. From the fulcrum of her crotch on up she was a stunning woman. Miss Macau Third Runner Up, Gretchen said. Or was it Veronique. Four years ago. And then there was that leg.

The Orion was a hangout for writers and artists who had stayed on after the Crash had sent so many others scurrying. There were booths along one wall for intimate conversation on topics writerly and artistic and a bookshelf with books on it. Jack Spoar was sitting alone at the far end of the bar. He could not lift his big schooner of draft beer to his lips without spilling it. He simply stared at it like a man with the shakes. Only once had I seen anyone that bad off—after the running of the bulls in a small town in southern Spain. Not even Pamplona. Still bulls are bulls. They were not any smaller in a small town.

"Jack," I said.

I was next to him on the barstool now. I did not want to sneak up on him. He was that bad off.

"So this is where you disappeared to."

"I went outside to run over my lines."

"We missed you."

"Out by the gondola landing. Next to the Tsunami Evacuation Route sign. I saw something in the dark. An ape or something."

"It's almost Halloween for Christ sake."

"Its eyes glowed in the dark. A night creature or something."

"Were you smoking anything?"

"A toke or two, sure."

"Well?"

"I wasn't high."

"You weren't high."

"I wasn't."

"Okay."

"And it spoke to me."

"Sure. *Trick or Treat.*"

"Some sort of gibberish."

"Wonderful language, that—Gibberish."

"Yeah. It gibbered and slapped at the sign post."

"Imagine that," I said.

"And made a lewd gesture."

"Gave you the finger, eh. When you didn't give it any candy."

"I wasn't high."

"Drink up."

"I'm trying to."

Ms Grabor-Hepinstall came over and bought me a draft beer. She was with a Lesbian poet friend. The Lesbian poet friend did not like me because I had once told her my favorite Lesbian poet was Dorothy Parker. This did not set well. I had no idea whether Dorothy Parker was a Lesbian or not. I just liked her because she was funny and a world class drunk. I was just shooting off my mouth and deserved the cold stare I got.

"That was a good line about steak tartare and eating pussy," Sheila said.

"You were at the Open Mike tonight?"

"Vivienne told me."

"Actually," I said, "I read it somewhere. A writer said it. I stole it."

I wanted to ask what pussy tasted like to her—as a Lesbian. I really wanted to know. I might could splice it into the routine. Then I thought better of it. It felt like one of those nights when even the slightest slip of the tongue might be taken all the wrong way.

"Good," she said. "So I can use it in a poem."

I shrugged and smiled. "Sure. You can dedicate it to me."

"Okay," Sheila said. "Why not," and she shot me a look of withering and imperial condescension.

"Oh my God," Ms Grabor-Hepinstall gaped raptly at the door of the Orion. "They're here!"

The Insider couple had come in with the Alien in tow. The Insiders towered over everyone in the place like the only adults in a room full of schoolkids. They moved easily in the crowd. If you have ever seen a two masted yacht glide into a harbor with a lot of smaller boats bobbing around it, that is what they looked like.

"Look at *her*," Sheila gasped. She was nearly out of breath.

The male Insider, I will call him Giorgio—I did not learn this till later—Giorgio went over to the bar and said something to Tommi and she rang the brass ship's bell above the bar three times and this meant drinks were on the house for the next half hour. There was applause and some "Yays!" and the girls behind the bar began pouring shots and putting them on trays or just sliding glasses across the bar. A shot of clear liquor appeared in front of me and I tossed it down and Jack Spoar did the same with his shot of tequila. He lifted it to his lips and was able to get it into his mouth and this evened him out some.

I turned around and the Alien was in my face. It hissed viciously.

"Get the Pythoness out of here now! And her damned bottom feeder boyfriend with her."

"That's not my call. Anyhow they're my friends."

"Get her out of here."

"Get them out of here yourself, Justine."

The Alien glared at me. Or rather its window glared at me.

"Don't call me that in here or anywhere else."

"I'll call you anything I want."

"You want her with *two* gimp legs?"

"Jesus. You talk like a fucking gangster."

I slid off my barstool and stormed toward the door. Outside it was cool and clear and I walked along a sandy path with scrub on both sides. I walked until I could no longer hear the music from the Orion. There were some lights up ahead and I followed them to an open air snack stand on the beach side of the path. I sat down in a plastic chair at a rusting iron table. Nobody was around. Finally Old Santana came out and I ordered a beer.

"Alone tonight?" he said. "No girl?"

"When was the last time you saw me here with a girl?"

He shrugged and returned with the beer. Maybe he had taken me for somebody else.

"Old guys got to get laid too."

"Cheers," I said.

"Jesus," he said.

At the edge of the pool of the snack stand's lamplight stood the Insider male and the Alien. The Insider was smiling. It might have been the poster for an old sci fi movie and for an instant I had the creepy sensation I had been in just this situation before. The Insider standing just where he was and the Alien next to him just where it was and Old Santana gaping at them. The brain hiccup passed but not the chill of bewilderment.

"If you prefer to be alone we'll turn back."

Outside of the two nude goddesses on the wall that night, it was the first time I had heard an Insider speak. The voice was hushed and confident and irresistible as if he were ordering a bottle of expensive champagne from a wine list. The Hazmat suit of the Alien was accordioned at the knees and waist and elbows like the neck of a jack in the box head. Before I had thought it was just ill fitting but now it seemed deliberate.

"May we approach? Someone here owes you an apology."

"If she takes off that damned headpiece."

"You can open your visor, darling," the Insider said mildly. "For five minutes only."

They stepped forward into the full glare of the overhead lamplight. The face of Justine inside the headpiece looked swollen—almost bloated—babyish save for her heavy black eyebrows and thick sensual lips. But the filmy veil was gone. She was smiling a little, squinting. They did not sit down.

"Okay," I said.

"Go ahead, doll."

"I'm sorry, Harold. That shrieking bitch Gabriela just flew at me in the Patio. I couldn't protect myself in this outfit. She wanted to rip my face off."

"Gabriela?" I said.

"Your Pythoness," the Insider helped us out.

I stared at them. They could not even get her name right.

"What was going on?" I said. "What did you say to her?"

"Nothing. Absolutely nothing. She called me a Slut. A Freak. You heard her. Everybody did. The nerve of that damned little gimpalope."

"A cat fight," I said. "A fucking cat fight?"

"Well, I'm sorry," the face of Justine said. "And for screeching at you in the Orion."

"Mr. Ranter," the Insider said and extended a palm.

"Ratner," I said. We did not shake.

"Rather. Quite right. Awfully sorry. My name is Giorgio. Paleologos. I am looking after our friend."

I wanted to swing on him. I don't know why. I had no right to. No, I do know why. It was that "looking after" that got me. And that patronizing "our friend." What checked me I do not know. No, of course I know. He was well over a foot taller and rangy through the shoulders. And I did not want to be flattened by a Mr. Politeness in a navy blue polo shirt.

"Giorgio," I said. "What kind of a gigolo name is that?"

The Insider named Giorgio smiled. "Well, at least you didn't call me a pimp."

"Guys!" the face of Justine said. "I can't keep this visor open all night. My face is starting to swell up more."

"Then shut it!" we both said. It was almost laughable and certainly embarrassing. We drew back.

"Mr. Ratner, the two of us would like to invite you on a little outing. Wednesday, say. Elevenish. Or whenever you are free. You have never been on one of our airships. Blue Hole Tour. Just the three of us. You will want to see the island from up there before you leave."

"Leave," I said.

"I told you he was stubborn," the headpiece hissed its Alien hiss. She had shut her visor. "The only one who won't go."

"We'll see. We'll see if we can't make the old sport a gangplank offer he can't refuse."

X.

Rudolfa pressed the tips of both thumbs into the ball of my foot. This would deliver a jolt of healing energy to my liver which she was certain I was abusing because I was not married and did not pay for a Special. Rudolfa was among the last remaining big island gals of the contingent who had come to the island a decade back when the hotels were full of tourists and positions for housemaids went begging and you could pick up 500 escuchos now and again on the side when a guest rang up room service for an extra set of clean towels. Lots of rich people came in those days. VIPs too. Movie stars. Rock stars. Yachts anchored out in the bay. She thought Chelsea Clinton would win in November and that her two divorces and her affair with her chauffeur were her own business and nobody else's. And still so young looking—for a woman pushing seventy. Not a day over thirty. She's rich, I said. They can do that now. Rudolfa believed the iguanas on the island housed evil spirits and would not go near one. Their eggs are okay to eat because the evil spirits do not enter their bodies until after the baby iguanas hatched. That male iguanas have two penises is just more proof of their malevolence and an attribute of Satan besides. Maybe they fucked the female iguanas in the pussy and asshole at the same time like her ex.

"Joker fucks iguanas?" I said.

"No," she paused and considered this. "That is where he draws the line."

Rudolfa asked me for the umpteenth time why I was not married. She remembered Justine. Justine had such creamy olive skin. Such raven hair. And still so young, Rudolfa said. In my twenties I had hair of such richness too. She had not really killed herself, had she. No, Rudolfa was certain she had not. Such a sin. The one thing God could not forgive. She liked the new Pope in Rome. At first she was shocked he had come out as a gay man. But if you thought about it it made sense. Leonardo da Vinci was gay. Or was it Michelangelo. Her cousin was a nun and had been to Italy. The cousin had seen the statue of David and it had spoken to her. The cousin would not reveal what the statue said. She would reveal it only to the Pope and only if the Pontiff asked. But the statue had spoken in Latin, that the cousin would reveal. David was a Hebrew, I said. He would not talk in Latin. Rudolfa thought about this long and hard. She was on my other foot now. Why your big toe sticks out like that, Rudolfa said. Like hitch hike thumb. It's abducted, I said. Don't bullshit me. It's still there. Just sticks out. Harold knows the Pythoness, does he not. Indeed Harold knows the Pythoness. The Pythoness has one good foot and one that is distorted. They do not match. Mine did not match either but the Pythoness's feet do not match much worse. The Pythoness came here for a massage? Not exactly. Rudolfa had given her a pedicure, not a massage. What is wrong with her jaked leg? Rudolfa did not know. The Pythoness would not talk about it. But it had not always been that way. She was not born a gimp. That Rudolfa was certain of. Probably an accident. A punishment for overweenie pride.

Overweening, I said. Okay, Rudolfa said. That's just what people said. She made a mistake and had to pay for it. What was her mistake? Probably pride in her beauty, Rudolfa said. Vagina hubris, I said. What, Rudolfa said. You have to pay for things. Nothing comes for free.

"You can say that again," I said.

"You want hand job? 500 escuchos only."

"Sorry. I'm a little short."

"Ha! You are funny. Okay 300 escuchos for short guy. 100 escuchos for one inch."

"I didn't mean that."

"That's okay. Just kidding. Anyhow your friend paid for you already."

"What?"

"Insider friend. He came by last night. With Alien. Paid 2000 escuchos."

"You're joking."

"Just in the case you came in."

"The pimp!"

"Shush."

"Then give me half."

"No!"

"You want me to tell him you tried to hit me up for 500 escuchos? When he already paid you."

"No."

"Suit yourself then. 1000 escuchos."

"Some people say Insiders gimp her leg," Rudolfa said darkly.

"What?" I said.

"Nothing. Here."

Outside of the Happy Ending it was hot in the sun. It was like stepping out of the depths of a cathedral. I thought better of what I had said inside and went back in and gave Rudolfa my share of the escuchos back. I knew I would think about what I had done all day and kick myself for it. It was not my money. I had not earned it. You want hand job now, Rudolfa said, and we laughed.

At the canal a gondola drifted up. Funny how you never saw them around until you needed one and then one was there. Like they were following you around just out of sight. The gondolier was smoking a joint. He shrugged when I asked if he wanted a fare.

"The museum," I said.

"It's Monday. Closed."

"I know," I said.

"You wanna buy some pot. Good stuff. Not Emporium medicine bullshit."

"No thanks."

"You don't smoke?"

"Okay. Give me a couple of joints."

I was half expecting a sleepless night. The gondolier stopped the gondola and carefully rolled two.

"Make them fat ones."

"Fattest on the island."

"How much?"

"50 escuchos each."

"Jesus."

"Yep," the gondolier said. "You smoke these you see

crazy shit. Jesus. Monkeys. Aliens."

"You seen any Aliens?"

"Sure. Last night. Here. Same place. Tall guy too. Insider maybe."

"Where'd you take them?"

The gondolier clammed up.

"100 escuchos. Two joints."

"Where?"

"They sat in front. Very romantic. Alien gave him blow job maybe. Homos maybe."

"I don't think so." The gondolas were not wide. Barely enough room to seat two abreast in the front—not enough for a "tall guy" and someone in a Hazmat suit. Maybe she just sat on the floor between his legs and stared ahead. Certainly she just sat on the floor between his legs and stared ahead.

"So what are Aliens anyway—men or girls?"

"They're Aliens," I said sharply.

The gondolier shrugged.

"Where did you take them?"

The gondolier gave me a weary look.

"Don't remember. Everybody on this island crazy now."

"Yeah. From smoking your shit."

"Yep." He was smiling now.

"Where are you from?"

"Here and there."

"Mostly there, huh."

"Mostly there."

The gondolier offered me a toke off his joint but I declined. We glided past a splendid frangipani with its pink blossoms and some bougainvillea creeping and climbing. On the face of the black water floated orange and yellow petals of flowers whose names I had been too careless to learn. It was right around here one afternoon Justine claimed she had spotted a blue beaked bucolic eyecatcher frolicking among the lianas, and covered her face. When I shouted Where? Where? and covered my face too, she burst into such a shower of cackles that even our sullen gondolier stared at us in bafflement. Beyond all this efflorescence lurked the disused clubhouse of the golf course that had long gone ungroomed. It was fenced in now with a sign on it but I could not read the sign through the foliage. The canals themselves had once served as sources of irrigation and had watered its fairways and greens. The gondolas and their pilots ferried foursomes back and forth between the hotels and the 19th Hole Bar. The tourist brochures raved about this Venetian touch and the footbridges that arched over the canals and the stroke of entrepreneurial good sense that banished automobiles and trucks from the island. Nobody missed the car salesmen when they packed up and left. Well, the whores at Aye, Claudia's did, of course. Gretchen stood on the ferry slip staring out to sea for two full days until Yumi and Veronique dragged her back to the bar again. Even in a perfect world you cannot make everybody happy.

We pushed on past the shantytown that had sprouted up in the wake of the Crash. It was abandoned now except for three or four shacks. In front of one an iguana the size of a rabbit roasted on a spit over a bed of charcoal. With its legs stuck up in the air it did not look like it had put up much of a fight. The iguanas had been brought to the island as pets but escaped and had thrived. They were not native to the place. They were an invasive species, technically speaking, through no fault of their own. There was even a small bounty on them if you brought their heads in. They were not hurting anything. In fact they were part of the island's lore—with their two penises and all. And their eggs hard boiled were not bad with beer. A little cheesy, sure. Some wags held that they were aphrodisiacs though they just made me flatulent the next morning.

A young woman with a shallow woven basket of yellow mangoes on her hip eyed us coquettishly as we approached. Except for her yellow factory dress she might have just stepped out of a Gauguin. The gondola stopped and she got in and handed the gondolier a mango from her basket. She smiled at me and her teeth were like tiny pointed seeds and I looked away. Two men squatted behind the iguana on its spit and drank a cloudy brew from glass jars. They could have been thirty years old or they could have been sixty. One of them made us a lewd gesture but the young woman ignored them. She had brown skin like Rudolfa and thick black hair gathered into two braids down her back. Seated there in the gondola in her faded yellow dress she reminded me of butter for some reason. Or hot buttered rum. I have always tried hard not to feel bad for people who have nowhere to go back to. Sometimes it feels too much like pity.

"You live there?" I said and pointed at the shacks of the shantytown.

She stared at me.

"How much for a mango?"

She said nothing.

"One," I said and pointed at her basket.

She held up three fingers.

"No," I said. "Just one."

Again she held up three fingers.

"No. Just one."

"She means three escuchos. Deaf," the gondolier said. "And dumb."

XI.

Angry Stan Panik ran the little canalside museum attraction with its dioramas of the stunted and extinct original ape inhabitants of the island. He had inherited it from a distant uncle who died here of drunkenness and debauchery and an unhafted stone wedge between his shoulder blades. So we had our own Hobbit people just like the famous island ones over yonder—only ours had tail stubs and no stone tools at all. Technically they were not even human but we thought of them warmly. Darwin mentions them somewhere. Said they were promiscuous as hell. Shameless. He called the females nature's foremost miscreants, I think, and marveled at the histrionics and clownishness of the males. But we liked to believe they had lived in harmony and song and one of Stan's pride and joys was a skeleton of conjoined twins fused at the backbone. If they had survived to adolescence—and Stan claimed the partial eruption of their second molars demonstrated that they had—was this not proof of altruism and a general niceness. Something or somebody had kept them alive for a while. Whatever the case, both skulls are frozen in rictus grimaces of rage and terror. Others claimed Stan's uncle had gotten a shade too creative when he slapped the bones together that way. Maybe back in real life they were separate and hated the shit out of each other. Maybe that's why they are screaming now.

We filled the skulls with sand one day and measured the volume of the sand and compared it to what we thought the original body mass of the twins probably was. With these numbers we calculated it had a total IQ upwards of 70. So each brain by itself was about half the low end of average. Not bad for something that was not even human. Who knows what they might have achieved had they lived long enough and been able to pool their cunning.

The race had gone extinct when sailors in the nineteenth century brought syphilis to the island. Stan was certain he could detect this in the scarring on their bones. This seemed a flight to me but in the very last panel of the diorama a drunken Jack Tar has at a gracile female of the species who is presenting—her vulva velvety textured and shockingly human. A couple of steps beyond this a heavy upholstered door with a buzzer button leads to a sex toy shop operated by Stan's Thai wife. Beside the cash box sits a stack of business cards for the Happy Ending Massage Therapist half a mile up the canal. One thing leads to another, one guesses, in the evolutionary scheme of things.

And the stone wedge, we all thought, was a nice touch. It was from the uncle's own collection of island oddities. Perhaps one of the last apes had gotten a little inspired toward the end. Syph, they say, can do that. Van Gogh. Rimbaud. Manet. Nietzsche. Wilde. Perhaps the decadent old fart pitched backwards on it one drunken night in the dark. That was Angry Stan's story, anyways. Stranger things have happened here.

Indeed the museum was closed. The gondolier was right, of course. On the front door hung a sign that read CLOSED

ON MONDAYS with the ON MONDAYS crossed out. The front door would not open. Angry Stan was around back behind the museum with a long Grim Reaper scythe in his hands. He had mowed down half of his signature cannabis patch and was taking a breather. Saturday night at the open mike he had taken me aside and suggested I stop by. Soon. So here I was. He had sounded urgent and conspiratorial at the time. Now he just looked bushed.

"Glad you could come by."

"What's with the scythe," I said.

"Come on inside."

The interior of the museum was dark and Stan switched on a few lights. The floor had not been swept in a while. He had been losing money since the Crash as the tourists evaporated. It had hit the resort islands first and hardest. Almost immediately the package tours dried up. Then the better off started canceling. And canceling. Everybody stayed home and donned their virtual reality headgear and giggled themselves silly. The obscenely well heeled stopped appearing on the horizon, stopped anchoring out in the bay on their yachts. No doubt they had islands of their own anyways. We waited, hoped, prayed. Drank. Amazing how everything in the tropics can start to crumble around you in the space of just a few months. Then the Insiders showed up, a breed apart. No explanations. Just smiles a mile wide and arm spans like condor pinions. Anyhow, that's what Stan's garden out back was all about. Grow your own and pick up a few escuchos on the side.

"Beer," he said.

"Sure."

"Toke?"

"No thanks."

"Good."

There was a mini fridge behind the souvenir counter. He did not have to go upstairs.

"Look around," Stan said.

"Something new?"

"No. The opposite."

"Pardon?"

"We're closing. Closed. For good."

"No," I said. "Already."

"Take your pick," Stan said.

I looked around at the shelves and display cases. The ape hand in its bottle of preservative was nowhere among all the other oddities Stan's uncle had amassed. There was an empty space where the bottle was supposed to be. I had long coveted it for its humanness and the good shape it was in. Had even made Stan a joking offer for it once or twice. The museum was The Best Bad Taste Museum in the island chain and the hand was its centerpiece. The other stuff was good, sure. The Tahitian fertility sculptures and the Caribbean voodoo dolls. The Cyclops glass eye. The Ainu shaman wind skates. The Wrangel Island mammoth foot umbrella stand. The Sakhalin temple dancer mouse skull wrist bangles. The stuffed iguana with bat's wings (*Preguntasaurus paniki*). Anything with an island slant to it. To an expert the whole layout would have been risible—to the tourist an occasion for contemplation and enlightenment and awe. Robert Ripley had nothing on Stan's uncle.

"The hand," I said. "Where's the hand."

"That's gone."

"Gone? I thought I had dibs on it."

"They bought it months ago."

"They?"

"You know who. Our new friends from the far end of the beach. Told us to keep mum about it. Or else, they said. Just before they started stepping up the pressure on the last of us."

"Odd coincidence," I said.

"Indeed."

When they bought the hand, Stan said, they had bought him out. The museum was the hand—the hand was the museum. The whole place was just a junkshop without it.

"Damn," I said.

"I know," Stan said.

"How much did they give you?"

"A lot. Bullion ounces. Coins. Not fucking escuchos. More than the whole joint is worth."

"Rich bastards," I said.

"DNA freaks. That's what they are."

"What about the sex toys in back. Can I have my pick there?'

"What—is Miss Muffet lonely?"

"Good one," I said.

"We're taking that inventory with us."

On a pedestal in the middle of the room stood the museum's other real pride and joy. Stan had stitched half a dozen cows' tongues together in a ball and put it in a jar of formalin and labeled it: *Head of Blind Street Beggar, Rukuvuku, Oceania. Gift of: Oxfam.* There was a joke in there somewhere, I was sure, though I could never quite put a finger on it.

"You can have that," Stan said.

"I don't think so."

"It's a work of Art!"

"I know."

"They have an identical one in the Whitney. Fucker visited here one year and stole my idea. He just used horses' tongues instead."

"I just don't have anywhere to put it," I said.

"Take it," Stan said. "I just don't want those Insider bastards to sell it for a million bucks someday."

We finished our beers. It made me uneasy to be drinking in front of the Beggar, almost a sacrilege. Sometimes the place made you think.

Stan's wife came downstairs with a plate of snacks. She was an upcountry woman and very dark and had wonderful thighs. When we first met I did not think they would last, but they had. The thighs, I mean. She went by the name of Toom and this unnerved me a little. Of course in the Thai language it would not suggest anything sinister. It probably meant "precious joy" or "the Buddha's smile" or some other such blessedness. But her eyes behind those dark brown features blazed fiercely and her hint of a moustache gave one pause. The snacks were a delight: cheese and almonds and anchovies and shrimp Thai style. The anchovies were not good for my gout but that just made them the tastier.

"We're moving back to Thailand," she said. "Isn't it wonderful."

"I envy you," I said.

"There will be adjustments," she said. "We will have to make adjustments."

We talked about adjustments for a while. She wanted a child now. You could not have one on the island. Stan did not say anything. You could not tell what he was thinking. With the money from the sale of the hand they could make a start, she said. Stan seemed to agree with this. They would invest in a bar, maybe. I asked her if they would have whores in the bar. This was not a well advised comment. No whores. Good, I said. Well, she said. There would be girls of course. It would be up to them. But no bar fines. She and Stan would not make money that way. They were to be congratulated, I said. This did not come out right either and I regretted my words. Times are tough, I wanted to say, and I begrudge no one their choice of a livelihood, but wisely I shut up. Only a man who has fallen for a whore, I wanted to say. But I dared not finish the thought.

"They wanted the DNA," Toom said finally. "The hand's."

"Come again," I said.

"I overheard them talking. They didn't know I speak English. We play that game sometimes."

"Odd," I said.

"We knew you wanted it. But they made us an offer we couldn't refuse."

Stan nodded.

"Take the Beggar," she said. "Give him a good home. We

can't take him with us. The jar might break. And you can't carry on something like that."

"Yes," I said. It was hard to say no to her.

"Maybe he will bring you luck," Toom said.

"Take it," Stan said. "We're going to have one last HaHa Hole here and that will probably trash the place."

I woke up a couple of hours before dawn with a vague unease. The Blind Street Beggar stared down at me from my bedroom bookshelf. I had set him up there next to my backpack with its NO BOZOS logo stitched on the flap. There had been no smokes about the place for months, but I wanted one now. I lit a joint and peeled the mango and ate it. That took care of most of the day's booty. I got Miss Muffet out of the bottom drawer and caressed the pair of taut buttocks that she was and fondled the folds of her velvety vulva and thought about young Molly O'Healey and then Ms Grabor-Hepinstall. But that did not do the trick. I cast about and thought about the two goddesses I had seen on the wall but no soap. And so on and so on. I thought about the Pythoness who I had sworn to myself I would not think about this way and blessedly she limped out of sight. Her dippity gait had a weird aura of sanctity, I guess. Of Touch Me Not. I did not think about Justine. I am superstitious that way. It is that simple. An Iron Law. If I thought about Justine now I would never bed her again. Ever. I put Miss Muffet back in the drawer and patted her gently. It was not her fault I could not get off. Then I thought about Toom and her thighs and started to get aroused and took her out again. I was not going to do this all night, I told myself, and then I did not have to. Then I thought about what I was going to do with Miss Muffet when my time finally comes. I could not leave her here to be found by strangers. That would be too humiliating, even for a dead man. I decided I would decide again in the morning. That was enough to put me back to sleep.

XII.

Mr. Kang did not show up for class. His desk chair near the door stood empty.

"Maybe he eloped with the Pythoness," Molly said. She was serious. Ms Grabor-Hepinstall was not:

"For her mouse."

"Or her pussy!" Jack was back. He had recovered from his encounter with his ape. He was his old self again.

Molly blanched. Ms Grabor-Hepinstall scowled and shot him a dark look.

But the vulgarism was an opportunity to launch into the day's lesson on puns and double entendres and homophones and their inadvisability. Too bad Mr. Kang was not here. His English intonation was often a little off and when he wanted to say *elephant*, for example, it would come out *a leaf ant* and the conversation took an odd trajectory. Otherwise it was a dreary task—not less because I secretly relished a good pun and reveled like a masturbator in my own feats of paronomasia. I implore you to eschew puns in public, I said. Do it only at home, alone, doors closed. I quoted Dr. Johnson on Shakespeare and reminded everyone that a pun was the lowest form of humor. This wisdom was duly absorbed. At the same time I knew everyone in the room was equally absorbed in coming up with a pun that would hurtle us into squeals of delight. This was only human. But try to come up with a side splitting pun when you really want one. Even if you ran into a truly riotous one just a few days ago. See, okay, or even an unforgettable timeless classic: Asbergers. But try to come up with one of your own. Go ahead. Try it.

"Not so easy, huh?" I said. They were impressed. I had read their minds.

"Okay. Now try this." I scratched *new dance* on the blackboard. "Make it sexy and a little incestuous."

Minutes passed. The second hand on the clock in the back of the room swept blithely along. Harold the Schoolmaster.

"Nude ants!"

"Ants. How do you spell that, Molly?" I said

"A-N-T-S."

"Sorry. That's sexy—but hardly incestuous."

"Nude *aunts!*" Jack Spoar erupted. "A-U-N-T-S!"

"Bingo," I said.

We tackled pinnacle of (pinochle love), a few seek hay (f-u-c-k), bigger mistake (bigamist's steak), growing my take (groin might ache), Monday night rubble (mundane eye trouble), pick and choose (piquant shoes), we mentored ourselves (women toured arse elves), g-spot (jizz pot), Roar, Jacques! Tess! Steve! (Rorschach test eve), Aye, bid adieu to rest (I bit a dude tourist) and I gave them sheaf eels beat raid (she feels betrayed) and jocose seer (joker's ear) for homework. Then I added The sky god who cares (This guy got hookers) if just to needle Ms Grabor-Hepinstall a little.

We talked about near puns. Or are they half puns. We talked about them philosophically. People never really listen to each other. We seldom do. We hear only half what other people are saying, they said. The surface half. Right,

I said. My husband, Ms Grabor-Hepinstall began. Then she stopped. She did not finish her thought. We all grew pensive. We were stuck in halfness. We all knew where we were going but we could not figure out how to get there from here. Still, I said, half puns can be great fun. Allow me to illustrate. On the blackboard I sketched a cartoon figure shaped like a hot dog with stick arms and legs. He is staring at a letter he has just removed from an old fashioned rural mailbox. The kind with a little metal flag on the side that goes up and down. Underneath this I captioned: *You may already be a wiener.* Molly tittered. I do not know if she got it or not. Maybe it was just the idea of a wiener that got to her. Here's another one, I said. A poem. Before anyone could object that it was almost lunchtime I wrote it on the blackboard in neat block letters. It's by a guy who died behind iron bars, I said. For dismembering his faithless lover. I thought a gruesome murder might make it more intriguing. In fact I had knocked the thing out that morning. It filled one big square of the blackboard and spilled over onto the next:

PARADISE

So I pick up this gal
at the Patio
not much English
a little skinny
hint of a limp
but a nice gal

just the same
and take her back
to my place
pour us each
a glass of chianti
and tell her about
my dream: a villa
with a view of Lake Como
over a splendid piazza
and she says Yeah
with pepperoni and
mushrooms

"I'm hungry," Jack Spoar said. "I know what she means."

"It's so sad," Molly said. "Depressing."

"With tomatoes and anchovies," Ms Grabor-Hepinstall said. "Sounds better." She hung out with poets and imbibed their preferences.

"What about the joke?" I said.

"Great," Jack said flatly.

"Funny," Molly said flatly.

"Heard it before," Ms Grabor-Hepinstall said flatly.

What would Mr. Kang have thought, I wondered abstractly, and attacked the board with my eraser.

In the men's room McPheeters was bellied up to the urinal by the window, his kilt hitched up to his waist and its sporran nudged to the side. I took the urinal at the opposite end of the bank. On the wall in front of my nose some wag had scrawled:

Alone tonight?
Christian Escorts:
Dial R-A-P-T-U-R-E

Not bad. Jack Spoar, perhaps? No, not Jack. Justine maybe. Maybe Justine. She was a whiz at the six word story: *At Lovers Leap paused. Reconsidered. Split.* And: *Molotov cocktail dresses. Ideological cleavages exposed.* And: *Sasquatch retires. Gorilla suit for sale.* And: *Stadium Bobblehead Day: Bring kids. Hatchets.* We stayed up all night once until we ran out of paper. McPheeters finished his business and let his kilt drop and arranged it carefully.

"Got a minute?" he said.

"Sure. I just sent my class of clowns off to their pizza lunches."

"Good. Got a bottle of the real stuff."

In his office McPheeters poured me a tumbler of Macallan and then suited himself. On the coffee table lay an open book of photographs of old statues and some busts. Ancient Greece, it looked like. Praxiteles, the chapter title read.

"Good God," I said.

"What's that?"

"This guy."

"That's Hermes. Holding his little brother Dionysus."

"I know him."

"It's famous."

"No," I said. "I mean it. I've seen him."

"He is on one of your old American coins. A dime, you call them. With wings on his head. And fasces on the back."

92

"I met him. Saturday night."

"Handsome devil, no?"

"You've seen him too?"

McPheeters lifted his tumbler of whiskey.

"That's where this came from."

"Don't tell me. He made you an offer you couldn't refuse."

McPheeters nodded.

"Four days," he said. "They're giving me until Saturday. They are assholes. But generous. Looks like they're in a hurry. Giving people the bum's rush. Something's afoot. Anyhow the Long Pig is already shut down."

"Four days," I said. "So soon?"

"Oh come now. We've always known the day was coming."

We sipped from our tumblers and savored the scotch. Oak, we agreed. You can't beat oak. Can't beat it. The Insiders made no secret they were taking over. They had bought one whole end of the beach. The beach was public land. You could not buy it. But they did. It was easy. They first bought the people who they then bought the beach from. They bought the rest of the island from the banks. Who owned the banks. They owned the banks. What the banks did not own they bought anyhow. They did not lean on people. They did not need to. Since the Crash their money did not talk. It SHOUTED and no one was out of shouting range.

This Project Repristination, McPheeters said. He filled our tumblers again with the ambrosia. Oak, we agreed again silently. With a hint of sherry. Whiskey telepathy. That's what I don't get, he said. Repristination, I said. I don't know that word. It's in the dictionary, McPheeters said. Have you been up by the golf course. They fenced it off. Hung signs up that say PROJECT REPRISTINATION KEEP OUT. No, I said. I saw no such signs that said that. Look, McPheeters said. Open your eyes. Well it's their land now, I said. Yes, McPheeters said. Now. When are you leaving. I can't leave, I said. Nowhere to go. It's that young woman, isn't it, McPheeters said. No, I said. This is damned good scotch, isn't it, I said.

"One more thing," McPheeters said.

"What's that?"

"They found a body on the beach this morning."

"A body?"

"Some old snack stand geezer found it. Woman. Ugly mess."

"Drowned?"

"You could say that, I suppose. Leg mangled. Like someone tried to twist it off. Mouse stuffed down her throat."

"No," I said.

"Sorry. Friend of yours?"

"Something of a loner. But we got along."

"Somebody means business," McPheeters said.

*

"I am going," Miss Soobiah said.

"So I see," I said.

"Sooner than expected."

She had gathered up her things from the desk and stuffed them in her big over the shoulder bag. The corner of the makeup mirror she examined her lipstick in every afternoon peeked out of the top of the bag.

"They paid for my ferry ticket. And then my flight home to Mauritius. Hotel rooms too. Something for my parents. They are very generous."

"I am sorry I can't give you anything," I said. My head was still buzzing from McPheeter's scotch. If I had anything more than the fifty escucho note in my wallet I would have given it to her.

"I liked working for you. In spite of you were always staring at my boobs."

"I am sorry about that," I said feebly.

"If you weren't so much older than me," she said.

"I am still a man."

"I know," she said. "You think everything revolves around you."

"Occupational hazard," I said. "I'm a comedian."

"I know. And it's okay to be an asshole up on stage. Just not in the office too."

"Well, I hope you meet your Prince Charming someday."

Miss Soobiah fell silent. I had not meant to sound sarcastic. She set her bag back on the desk and sat down in her chair. Her eyes glistened and a fat teardrop welled up but refused to release itself. This was a side she had never revealed. Her calm efficiency and impervious glare of toleration had evaporated. This was no longer the Miss Soobiah of the concentrated gaze at her notebook screen and unflappable rejoinders to my boob jokes.

"I met him already," she said.

I said nothing. I did not want to break the chain of her thoughts.

"He talked like he was way old and wise. But he couldn't have been more than twenty five."

"Go on," I said.

"He said if I didn't have a ridiculous glug glug laugh like Popeye maybe he could do something with me. Make me an offer I couldn't refuse."

"Your laugh?"

"A smarter laugh. A more sophisticated laugh."

"What a cruel thing to say," I said.

"Yes," she said. "He said they don't do voices. Or fingerprints or irises. The tell tale things. Probably he was just pulling my leg. But he sounded so—sincere."

"Was his name Giorgio?"

"Still he was so—*nice*. I couldn't say no. And what a huge thing he had. I felt like that queen the horse fell on."

"Was his name Giorgio?"

"And crushed her," she said.

"You'll be missed," I said.

"Whatever," Miss Soobiah said, and finally the tears began to roll.

XIII.

A shadow passed soundlessly over the shallow concrete terrace outside the kitchen window of my bungalow. The late morning was cloudless. An iguana sat on its tree limb unblinking. It was light green and then it was dark green and then it was light green again. That was probably a good day's work for an iguana. The Kaminskys next door toted their belongings out to the street and the movers loaded them into the back of the electric van.

I stepped outside to see if I could give them a hand. Some boxes lay in the sand and sparse island grass we called a lawn. One box was full of masks and had not been sealed up yet. Kaminsky and the other artists made a nice little killing every year in the run up to Halloween peddling their hand crafted papier mache masks to the tourists. Halloween was the signature holiday of the island back before the Crash and figured colorfully in the resort brochures.

"Take one if you like," Kaminsky said. "Old time sake and all that."

I looked them over. For a moment I thought he had said "old times ache." I was still hearing things homophonically.

"This one?" I said.

"Sure."

It was an ape mask.

"Friend of mine saw some guy wearing one last weekend," I said. "Ape suit too."

"Don't know about the suit. But I made a bunch of the masks. Got the idea from the museum diorama."

"Thanks," I said. I put the mask on and adjusted the eye holes.

"Can I do anything, Igor," I said.

"Naw," Kaminsky said. "Isn't that blimp thing waiting for you?"

The Ganymede: Blue Hole Tour hovered half a dozen yards in the air, its gangway extruded down and not quite resting on the asphalt of the disused parking lot of the Long Pig. It was a pint size version of the massive luxury dirigible airships that ferried the crowds of Insider vacationers over from the airport on the big island or long hauled them from Mykonos or Mallorca half a world away and docked at the tower inside the walls of the Casbah.

A Hazmat suit Alien stood at the foot of the gangway.

"You're late," the Alien hissed.

"I'm here," I said.

We glided up the gangway. The ride was like a conveyor belt without the escalator hum and rumble and vibrations. There was no handrail but you felt no fear of toppling off the stair, it was that smooth. Add an extra "oo" to that: smooooth. You felt a little like you were going down though you knew you were really going up.

The gondola seated a dozen—six on a side so that each passenger had a big window and an unobstructed view. The seats were too deep for me and the high cushioned backs too high and I had to stand up to see out my window properly. I was glad we were alone and there was nobody else there to see me. It dawned on me how the Pygmies must have felt when they arrived at the capital to petition the authorities to stop the anthropologists from pestering them with so many pointless questionnaires.

When the Ganymede lifted off there was no sense of the gravitational tug you sometimes feel on an elevator lurching into its climb. We rose like you are supposed to rise into the heavenly host painted on the inside of the cupola of a dome on a cathedral. *This gives us wings*, I remembered reading somewhere. Damned poets got it right sometimes. Though it might have been a magazine ad for those shoes that enable you to dunk a basketball over the head of some Promethean defender. Had Wilbur and Orville Wright run a novelty balloon shop back in Dayton, Ohio, and had an adequate supply of helium we might have spared ourselves the terror of bumpy runways and exploding tires and jetliners mishearing control tower instructions. And what do airships do if they thump into each other anyway: *Oops, sorry, man, didn't see you there. Catch you for a drink later in the Led Zeppelin off Concourse D.*

"Harold!" the Alien hissed. "You're drifting."

"Justine," I snapped. "Take off that damned headpiece."

"Giorgio?" the Alien hissed.

"At your discretion, dear."

Dear, I thought, but did not say anything. The most volatile synapse in the universe is the one between the brain and the tongue.

"At my discretion, Harold," the Alien hissed haughtily, as if I were deaf. "And take off that stupid ape mask. And don't call me Justine."

"After you," I said and we stared at each other—ape and Alien, Alien and ape.

The Ganymede skirted the coast of the island as we ascended and glided over the big sand dredger below. It was flat and broad and rectangular as a football pitch junked up with toy yellow power shovels and long sections of suction pipe looped back on each other like intestines with fiery red centipede heads and piles of brown sand destined for the beach extension and a battery of white tanks for fuel or potable water and tiny blue painted steel boxes where I guessed the workmen bunked and messed and drained their green bottles. The whole thing looked like a circuit board put together by Christmas elves with a flair for the improbable. On the beachfront of the Casbah sunbathers stretched out on the sand. The shadow of the airship slid over them like a pool of gray essence—neither air nor water. Engulfing them and then releasing them—caressing them almost. It gave one a surprising sense of power. Were they looking up and shading their eyes with one hand, you wondered, and waving with the other? You could not tell just as you could not tell if they were naked or not. You could not even tell if they were men or women from this height. How microscopic our sexual organs must appear to the eyes of the gods. And such a huge deal to us with our jokes and theories and lusts and longings and ribald tales of thwarted and doomed couplings.

We did not pass over the walls of the Casbah proper. This was a disappointment. Everyone wanted to know what it looked like inside there, even if just from the air. What was going on down there with our naked eyes. The girls who had worked there as hairdressers and housemaids and masseuses had stayed there day and night. They did not come out save to see their families who ferried over from the big island once or twice a month. The family members were quite mum about the whole business. And quite free spending in the days after the family visits. Dollars, too. Not escuchos. The shopkeepers smiled and rubbed their palms together when they saw them turning the corner. When the prettiest of the housemaids came out and confessed to her mother that she was three months gone there was a fuss. She disappeared again behind the walls and was said to have croaked in a tragic accident along with her unborn brat. Those were McPheeters' words, not my own. A ceiling collapsed as she lay abed, for God's sake, he sniffed. Fancy that. That was the story anyhow. The family was inconsolable. McPheeters was involved in the negotiations and almost blew any settlement at all. The family dismissed him and soon after the Insiders coughed up ten times their asking price. In dollars. Bullion. Gold coins. Not escuchos. Clever bastards, he told me. Slick sons of bitches. Fucking beautiful humiliation freak bastards with their ubermensch genomes and billion dollar designer babies. One moment they are charming the hell out of you and the next they are chopping your legs out from under you. Losing the commission was a bite, he said, but I suspect it went deeper than that. I ran my ass ragged, he said, which was amusing what with the kilt and sporran and sock garters and leather lapels like a pair of long drooping mule ears and the three hundred pounds of muscle and fat he carried on his lumbering frame. And it was not long before all the big island girls were sent packing. They stayed mum about the whole business. Paid off, almost certainly. Scared shitless, no doubt. It was about then we first noticed the Hazmat suits. We thought they were there to clean up some sort of toxic mess, but that end of the beach was always spick and span. Then Toby tagged them as Aliens, and that stuck too, and it got to be fun to but half believe it.

The run up to the Hole would take the better part of an hour, Giorgio said, if we cruise along at a couple of knots. He sat at the instrument panel in a captain's chair that recalled something you might find in an air terminal VIP Golden Gondola Lounge where you lean back and drift off and wake up at your destination. Not that I have ever been so lucky. The instrument panel looked more complicated than I imagined but I did not walk over to examine it. I did not want to seem impressed by the gadgetry, though a sort of linear gauge with a picture of a turtle at one end and a rabbit on the other puzzled me. The Ganymede topped out at seventy knots, he went on, though I had forgotten what exactly a knot was since my cruise ship days. A sluggard compared to the massive dirigible luxury liners that sail blithely along from ocean to ocean under calm skies at three hundred and fifty knots. Oh, really, I said. My. I did not want to encourage him in his smug, self satisfied prattle. Is Justine, I said, going to give us hum jobs along with the champagne and macadamia nuts? A sudden blow from behind snapped my head sideways and my ear stung and throbbed and the interior of the gondola went blurry for a second.

"You son of a bitch, Harold!" Justine screeched. Her headpiece was off now and she glared at me from the aisle. "You bloody fucking little son of a bitch."

Her face was furious but the old swelling had gone down and she was devastatingly lovely all over again—her eyes more lustrous, her sable Ishtar mane richer, her Temple Harlot lips even more bitter and searing and rapacious than our first insane nights together.

Giorgio was laughing. He swiveled in his captain's chair back and forth from the instrument panel to us and back to the instrument panel again. He could barely contain himself. The whole scene was too much for him.

"Hell of an alley cat, isn't she, Harold."

"Can't you see we're doing you a favor," Justine cried almost pathetically. "None of you people get to go up in one of these things."

"You pack a hell of a wallop," I said. My ear still smarted but Giorgio's hilarity made everything seem a little idiotic.

"We're doing you one last favor. Can't you see that? Giorgio was nice enough—"

"One last favor," I said.

"You're leaving the island next week. That's final. You can be the last to go. Nobody cares. Nobody gives a shit. But going you are."

"The hell I am," I said.

My ape mask had flown off with the blow. I picked it up off the floor of the gondola and put it back on. There was nothing more to be said.

XIV.

On the map the island has the shape of a dog bone biscuit or, as Jack Spoar put it one morning in class, the headless torso of a quadruple amputee. The lava cave at the southern end of the island floods at high tide and gapes vacantly at the sea the rest of the time. There is a rock shelf inside with bones on it. A femur and a pelvis, anyhow, and some ribs, presumably from one of the old apes. No tales have grown up around this tableau. It is just there, like a key left in a drawer and forgotten about.

The Ganymede was not high up enough in the air to take in the whole breadth of the island though I would have liked to. We left the lava cave behind and coasted up the middle length of the island with the luxuriance of the palm trees below on either side like fields of shredded clover. I had once watched a barefoot big island girl scoot up the slant of a palm trunk like a monkey and held my breath. She was a coconut gatherer and would lose her life before she lost her beauty which in that village was at a very young age. She does not really belong in this story but I am putting her in it here anyway. Maybe it was the ape mask on my face and the altitude.

Justine disappeared into the restroom closet at the rear of the gondola and emerged minutes later in a snappy flight attendant outfit. She must have had it on underneath the Hazmat suit. The navy blue blouse and charcoal gray slacks matched Giorgio's navy blue blazer and gray trousers. A silver blimp emblem pinned to her left breast announced GANYMEDE: BLUE HOLE TOUR. The getup was risible

104

but perhaps she was proud of her place in the new order of things. The pettiness of my crack about the macadamia nuts and hum job came home to me now. What had I ever had to offer her—a place up on stage by my side in the Roaring Twenties or the Holiday Sands saloon?

She stood taller now at the front of the gondola next to Giorgio as he maneuvered the shadow of the airship up this fairway and down that one. He seemed to be playing some private game of blimp shadow golf. The word *luftmensch* came to mind. McPheeters had used it once and shot me a scornful look. He liked foreign sounding words that nobody else understood.

"Giorgio drove the green on the sixteenth hole before it all ran to seed," Justine said.

"What are you talking about," I said. "That hole is 670 yards."

"Inches from the cup," Giorgio crowed. "Would've rolled in if the green had been kept up."

"Our Blue Hole is an average size blue hole," Justine began in a practiced sort of way. "Like our Sun is an average size star. You will see it on your left as we approach the eighteenth fairway."

I had seen it many times, of course, and hooked many a drive into it off the eighteenth tee, but I had never seen it from the air.

"As we approach you will note the dramatic contrast between the dark blue waters of its deep center and the light blue of the shallows around it. It is said to have no bottom. It is said to be nearly perfectly circular and to be bottomless."

"Bottomless," I said, and Giorgio laughed. For a moment we were brothers. Justine did not crack a smile.

"It is in fact over one hundred meters deep and about fifty meters across. It is fed by an underground spring. Nevertheless the water is anoxic. There is no oxygen in it. It can support neither aquatic nor marine life. There are no fish in it. No frogs. No turtles. The fossilized crocodile bones found nearby remain a puzzle."

We could see it now beyond the brow of trees lining the fairway. It was bluer from up here than from down below. Much bluer. Almost black in the center. Giorgio was maneuvering the airship toward it sideways, a neat trick, like docking a ship at a pier.

"It takes its color from the sky above and the white carbonate sand underneath. Some have compared the surface and depths of the water to the dark blue pupil and light blue iris of a human eye."

"Ready to watch it wink at us?" Giorgio said. "The sun is just right in the sky."

I stood speechless by my window. It was beautiful and just a bit terrifying. A single eye is not a comforting thing. Especially a liquid blue one, though I cannot fathom why. Some crazy story I read somewhere.

"The sun is at two o'clock," Justine explained. "Giorgio will now edge the shadow of the airship tangent to the circumference of the hole."

Another neat trick, and you imagined a load of passengers cued to erupt in applause as the opening bars of the old Space Odyssey number filled the gondola with its drums and horns and strings: *Hmmmmmm. Ta-da-DAH. Wuh-UH. BOOM boom BOOM boom BOOM boom BOOM boom BOOM boom BOOM boom BOOM.*

"Touche," Giorgio said.

"And now," Justine continued, "for the wink."

And wink the Blue Hole did. The shadow of the Ganymede crept across the span of the Blue Hole, paused tangent to its opposite bank, and retreated. It was both childish and a little lewd. Had I paid money for the tour—even escuchos—I would have felt like a sucker. On the other hand, the island had never looked so—alive.

"I don't think Harold's impressed," Giorgio said.

"I'm impressed," I said.

"You don't sound it. Jasmine, entertain the guy!"

"Jasmine? Who the hell is Jasmine?"

"That's my new name, Harold. I got it with the Upgrade. They just flipped a couple of letters. Like they do with your genetic code—they just flip a few letters and POOF you're an entirely new creature. A new phenotype. *Jasmine!*"

"Give the poor guy a break, Jas. Show him what you mean. Show him your—"

Giorgio gave the back of Justine's—JASMINE'S!—blouse a quick jerk and the blouse slid off her like a tablecloth in one of those stage magician's routines where the wine glasses barely shiver as the sheet of linen is yanked out from under them. Ole!

"—NIP!"

I stared in awe at the triumph of her boob job upgrade. She made a motion to cover herself but vanity trumped modesty as it ever does. Still something was not right and my eyes jumped from one breast to the other. The aureole on her left knocker was big as an old time half dollar and exquisitely chocolate cookied—but the other aureole was gone. It was not there. Her right breast was blind. I gaped at it like a suckling idiot infant that has been tricked by some mad scientist hidden behind a screen.

"Pretty discomboobulating, eh, Harold," Giorgio said. He laughed. He thought he was a riot. What kind of puerile comedy gene did these creatures have, anyway. I half expected him to whip out a canister of helium and launch into a Donald Duck imitation. And how dare him, I thought. Did he not know I came in third in an International Paronomasia and Homophony Slam in Montego Bay a decade back (and an honorable mention in Papeete three years later) when my star was still staggering into its brief ascent.

"They're winking at you," Giorgio said.

"What the fuck," I said.

"The gene for aureole size is different from the gene for breast size. That's why men can never get enough of tits," Giorgio explained. He sounded as rehearsed as Justine and I wondered if this too was part of the tour package. "Just like the gene for dentition is different from the gene for jaw size. That's why some people have crowded mouths like some Japanese women and others have those gaps between their choppers like the tops of castles. The trick for us was to split the symmetry and—"

"You've turned her into a sideshow freak!"

"She's not complaining. Are you complaining, Jasmine?"

She stared down at her chest and then looked at me.

"You never mentioned I'm taller, Harold. I'm two and a half inches taller. Three inches."

"I couldn't tell for sure with the floor of this thing tilting like that," I lied. The vanity of it all.

"Deck," Giorgio said. "It's a deck, properly speaking. This is an air*ship*."

"You never mentioned I'm taller," she sniffed

"They ruined your rack. They've turned it into a joke!"

"I'll be okay," she said. "As long as I never have twins."

"Jasmine is not only an Amazon," Giorgio said. "She's also an accomplished bombardier."

"Let's go back," I said. "I've had enough. You've ruined my one true love."

"Ha. You could have fooled us. You shit on her—what was it—back just before what you people call the Crash swept through here. The abortion. And the cheapo quick trip to Europe to make up for it. And then you dumped her. She told us all about it. Lucky for her she ran into us."

"I didn't dump her," I whined. "I cut her loose. There's a difference. There were no gigs. She was ready to go off on her own."

"Oh, and what about that Yuki babe?" Giorgio said.

"That was a fling. That's all it was. A man does that kind of stupid stuff when he's up against it all. I'm changed now. I've had time to think. I've changed."

"Good for you," Giorgio said.

He swung the Ganymede over the Blue Hole again, almost directly over it, and lowered the airship.

"Look down there," he said. "See those?"

I pressed my ape mask against the window to get a good look. On the bank of the Blue Hole sat three dark brown lumps. One of them moved with a sort of swaying, off balanced gait, like a hunchback. You could not tell if they were looking up or not.

"What are those things," I said.

"Apes," Giorgio said. "The crown jewels of our Project Repristination. Two males and a female. But that's okay. One's a little gay anyways. We couldn't help that. Dickhead Stavros forgot the second dose of testosterone. Yep," he said. "Let Nature take over again. With a little de-extinction help from Her friends. When we found the hand and saw it was the real thing we knew we could do something special with this place."

"Damn," I said.

"It's feeding time," Justine announced. She pulled a heavy sack from under one of the seats and dragged it to the door of the gondola. Her boobs swayed with the effort. I could not take my eyes off the blind one. I had seen pictures of nippleless jugs before but could not remember where—in a painting or something. Salamanders, I thought, those eyeless albino marine salamanders in the Lava Cave. They are like that too.

"They are full grown adults," Giorgio boasted. He was talking about the apes now. Not Justine's bazoombies. "Took us three months. Accelerated ectogestation. *In vitro veritas*. We brewed them fast in vats. Hope we got the pussy on the bitch right. Otherwise they may not mate."

"There was another one," Justine said. Jasmine—what the hell.

"Another one," I said.

"Another one," Giorgio said. "She lit out of the enclosure the other night. Had to cull her."

"Cull her," I said.

"Put the poor beast down."

"I see," I said.

"You have to," Justine said, and nodded. "If one steps out of line."

"Can't let them get too friendly with your kind in town," Giorgio said. "Don't want to spoil them."

"Our kind," I said.

"Sapiens sapiens. Don't take it personally."

"Then what the hell are you?"

"Jasmine," Giorgio said.

Justine pressed a button and the door of the gondola swung up and open gull wing fashion. She loosened the drawstring of the sack and took out mango after mango and let them slip over the doorstep. Down they plummeted through the air and entered the pupil of the Blue Hole and sank. I wondered what aerodynamic shape birdshit assumes once it has been released. Surely scientists must have studied that.

The apes did not stir at first. They just sat there. One by one the mangoes bobbed to the surface and caught the attention of the apes. That is what looked like was going on, anyways. They moved closer to the edge of the bank, waded in, and made a swim for it. In no time they were back on the bank with their armfuls of booty and munching away. Even from a hundred meters up in the air you could tell they were having the times of their lives.

"And now for the piece de resistance, Harold," Giorgio said. "Just for you."

"I don't think you will top what I've seen today," I said, and meant it.

"Jasmine," Giorgio said.

From the bottom of the sack Justine produced a glass bowl. It was empty. And unmistakable. I had seen it tons of times on the bar of the Patio.

"What's that," I said. "Where'd you get that?"

"Oh," Giorgio said. "Just something Jasmine found along the beach yesterday."

"Jasmine found—"

"A regular beachcomber, she is."

Justine held the bowl out the open door of the gondola and let it drop. We watched it glint in the sun and disappear into the center of the Blue Hole. The apes seemed to take no notice. They were too busy having the times of their lives.

"Mote in the eye that winked at you," Giorgio said.

"That's evidence," I barked. "You can't do that!"

"Harold," Justine said. "They just want you to know they mean business. That's all."

"You monsters," I said. "You murderers."

"Who's the monster?" Giorgio said. "You saw her leg."

"You did that to her. You people did it. I don't know how—"

"She did it to herself," Justine said. "She took her Hazmat

suit off before she was ready. Before she was fully Upgraded. It was her own fault."

"Harold," Giorgio said. "Let's change the subject. Nobody wants to play the blame game." He swung the Ganymede in the direction of the beach and we could already see the sand dredger offshore way in the distance. "What chance do you think I would stand up on stage?" Giorgio said. "Standup, I mean. Discomboobulating—that was pretty good, don't you think?"

XV.

Giorgio allowed me to debark the Ganymede on the beach in front of the Patio. We were out of the sanitized air of the gondola now and Justine was back in her Hazmat suit as the escalator extruded down. The boob show was over. She took my hand in her big Hazmat gloves and we shook. We had an understanding. Something was understood. Sometimes there are things you do not want spelled out. That are better left blurred. That you just don't want to be true. Still I wanted to say something bitter and hurtful but the right words would not come.

"Tell me one thing," I said. We were at the bottom of the escalator now. Out of the earshot of Giorgio.

"What's that?" she said. Her headpiece was not on. She had not put that back on.

"Why did Giorgio give the money to Rudolfa? What was the point of that?"

"I asked him to."

"But why?"

"I don't know."

"You don't know."

"I do know. I wanted to see him buy you."

"Buy me?"

"Oh, Harold," she said. "Shut up. Just shut up. Can't you just take a joke? Rudolfa, ha!"

"A joke."

"And I'll tell you something that's not quite so funny. We could have pushed you out that damned door too and you bloody well know it. Giorgio was ready to. Planned on it, in fact. He had me a little worried."

"A little," I said.

"Then the Pythoness didn't heed his warning to get the hell off the island pronto. That night at the Patio. And got her just desserts. So we just used the glass bowl. I talked him into it. You have no idea how close you came to walking the plank. You understand they mean business now, don't you?"

I looked up at the airship. The Ganymede. Could a vessel so sweetly named sport something so crude as a plank on it. Then I remembered what McPheeters said about the Pythoness. Her leg and the mouse. Did Justine try to talk them out of dispatching her so savagely.

"Justine," I said. "Jasmine."

"That's better. Now, Harold. Listen. They'll give you a little something to help set you up. More than enough to buy a little place on a lake somewhere. Fishing. A motor boat. Water skis. Maybe an island in the middle."

"A lake," I said glumly. "With an island in the middle."

"For god's sake, I've gone out of my way to get deals for everyone we know. Vivienne. Your pal Angus. Toby and Lorcan. Ruth Beth and Drago. The Kaminskys. The old crowd. Molly too. Even that moron Jack Spoar. Even your preeny Miss Soobiah from Madagascar or wherever. Thank god Giorgio listens to me sometimes."

"He fucked Miss Soobiah. Did you know that?"

"That was Stavros, ass wad. He loves assignments like that. She was lucky to have survived." Justine looked at me meaningfully. "The big island girl wasn't so fortunate."

"What? He fucked her to death? I thought a ceiling—"

"How you talk, Harold. Nobody *really* fucks anybody to death. At least not vaginally. Complications. Internal bleeding. And she wasn't even really pregnant. Just a little schemer. They say she was quite the Messalina. Belonged in Aye, Claudia's. Not—"

"YOU MEAN HE FU—"

"SHH. Get a grip, Harold. Hoppy will hear you. Anyhow it was before my time."

"Okay. Time to shut up," I said darkly. "But you know, Jasmine. You're not so funny anymore with your new name and boob job upgrade."

"Well if you're not careful you may end up the butt of one of their jokes."

"Like you?" I said.

Justine just stared. This one stung. I could see that. Touche, I thought, but whatever nerve the tip of my rapier struck rebounded with a shrug of weary and imperturbable nonchalance.

"I've got to get back aboard. This salt air is not good for my face. Nice chatting with you again, Harold. Ciao."

"Right," I said. "Chow."

"What's with the ape mask," Hoppy said.

He swiped at the bar in front of me and reset the napkin dispenser and the salt and pepper shakers and the jar of sugar.

"Just getting into the Halloween spirit of things," I said.

"No party this year."

"What."

"We're closing down."

"What else is new."

"Got a good deal. Last minute."

"Will wonders never cease," I said.

"Enough for a little place on a lake somewhere."

"Open a Bait and Tackle."

"Something like that. You heard about Graciela," Hoppy said. He was the only one of us who called her Graciela. To the rest of us she was the Pythoness. Old people are that way.

"When's the funeral?"

"No funeral."

"What are they going to do—hang her from a lamp post in the town square?"

"Jesus, what's got into you?"

"She died in my place."

"Your place? What are you talking about? They found her on the beach."

"Sorry. Had a bad day. Up in that blimp."

"What's it look like from up there," Hoppy said.

"Like a playground for apes."

"Huh?"

"Nothing," I said. "Never mind."

"Usual?" Hoppy said. "Chicken."

"With mashed potatoes and peas."

I took off my ape mask and set it on the bar. The novelty of the thing had long worn off. Hoppy disappeared into the kitchen. The kitchen was open air too and the odor of the charcoal smoke wafted up and down the beach. The three workmen from the sand dredger came in and took their usual table. Hoppy came back in and served them their little glass cups and green bottles and platter of grilled squid. He had not waited to take their order. They brought the squid in themselves sometimes and Hoppy took it into the kitchen and they let him charge them for grilling it on the charcoal brazier. A fair arrangement, Hoppy said. Even after a few glasses the workmen remained subdued, absorbed in discreet conversation. This was not like them. I tried not to listen in—my Korean would not have gotten me far anyhow—but the Pythoness loomed large in her absence. The youngest of the workmen stood up with some show of chair scraping upon floor and walked over to the barstool where she had always perched. He looked around in a way that announced he was looking around. He leaned over the bar and looked behind it. He felt inside the blind shelf under the bar and came up empty. At first I did not get it. He did not appear to expect to find anything there. Rather it was like some kind of dumbshow staged for my benefit. Koreans always had a flair for the dramatic. A peninsular people. The Italians, the kids on the cruise ship joked, of Asia. Finally he walked back to the table and sat down. My chicken arrived. I knew it was rude of me not to acknowledge them. Koreans have a rough code of warmth even for those they have met only casually. I had gotten a taste of this when the *Storm* put into Busan and my young friends from Food Service took me out on the town. But I was tired of people for the day. Let me eat my chicken and mashed potatoes and peas in peace.

And they almost did. My last forkful had nearly made it past my lips when the foreman—he of the white hard hat—was at my elbow. He set down a glass cup on the bar next to the ape mask and poured from one of the green bottles. He poured politely, as his countrymen do, placing the fingertips of his left hand high up on the forearm of his pouring hand. Please, *son-saeng-nim*, he said. It is good for the digestion. If we could have a word with you. When you have finished. If you would sit down with us. They disarm you, these guys, with their shy and careful deference. Bully you, really, in the no choice they give you. And *son-saeng-nim* means Honorable Teacher, or some such. I had heard it before. Honorable Foreman sat back down at his table and I made to pay my check. Hoppy waved me off and pointed at my tableful of friends. I had not seen that. Slick bastards. I was now in their debt. But I owed them one for the ride down the beach the other night too, I knew that.

The foreman was Mr. Kim. He was the one who had warned me not to hang out too long at the foot of the wall that night. The assistant foreman was Mr. Baek. Mr. Jang was the sand man. He sampled the sand. *Mo-reh.* The sand was good sand, clean sand. The island was a good island, we agreed. They were happy to meet me again. They had not been polite to me the last time. On the contrary, I said, they had been most accommodating. They had got me past the night guards with their purple fezzes. There was some translation going on by Mr. Jang but they were listening to me too. I appreciated the ride down the beach. They did not have to do it. Oh it was nothing. They did not know I was a teacher. If they had known, they said. I was a teacher of comedy, I said. That's all. And not a real teacher. They would not hear of this. They wanted to make up for their lack of consideration for me, a teacher. Would I like to visit their place of work. It would be an honor for them. That would be interesting, I said. But I am a little fagged out. I had a long day. No, not today. Of course not today. But tomorrow morning would be comfortable, would it not. They were leaving the day after. *Mo-rae*, the day after tomorrow. They were pulling out. The beach extension was finished. It was all done. They would like me to see it before they go. I had been curious about it, had I not. Indeed I had, I averred. Most curious. Good, then. Shall we send the buggy to fetch you. That will not be necessary. I will take a gondola. Be at the wall, then. By ten. Noon would be better, I said. There was some confabulation among the three. Some shaking and nodding of heads. Okay. Would there be sunbathers on the beach. Of course there would be sunbathers on the beach. There are always sunbathers on the beach. Do not worry. Good, I said. Oh, the foreman looked at me meaningfully. By the way. The *yoori jwee-jeep*. The glass mouse house. Did I know of its whereabouts. A strange question, I said. Yes, they said. They were sorry to trouble me about that. It is of no consequence, I said. I will keep my eyes open. That would be appreciated, they said. Tomorrow, then. Tomorrow, then.

XVI.

A sullen gondolier dropped me off in front of my office building. From there it would be an easy twenty minute hoof back to my digs if I took my time. There was no hurry.

"Where you going to go?" I said. It had only just struck me that these fellows too were soon to be sent packing.

"Nowhere to go."

"Back to your home country?"

"Home country," he said. "You a funny man."

"How much you getting?"

"Ha. Don't got nothing be compensated for. Shack not worth nothing. And I ain't none of their fancy whores neither."

"Huh," I said. "They're not giving you anything?"

"Ferry take us to big island. Then we on our own. Sons of bitches."

"I'm sorry," I said.

"That's five escuchos."

There was a light on in the window of McPheeters' room in the old Selkirk building. I walked upstairs and poked my head in his office door. He was putting books into cardboard boxes. Could I lend him a hand. We agreed I would just get underfoot. He knew where everything was to go. I watched him work for a few minutes, slipping the books carefully into place like a fisherman layering trout neatly into a creel.

There were two notes slipped under my office door. They were both folded up tightly into tiny hexagons Oriental fashion. The one from Ms Grabor-Hepinstall regretted I had not been in when she dropped by. She was leaving tonight on the ten o'clock ferry. She wanted me to know she liked me personally and that she had learned a lot in my classes. I was a good teacher and she understood my darkness was part of my brand of comedy. She did not think she had much of a future on stage but who knows, she said. She would see when she got back to Long Island. She hoped things might work out for me now that Justine was back—but quite frankly she did not think it likely. Giorgio was so very charismatic. He would be a hard guy to say no to. He could probably talk a nun out of her habit. That Stavros is something else though. Some words were crossed out here and I could not make them out. Why is it that they are the only ones you really want to read—the crossed out words. Anyhow she was sorry she had gone along with that classroom Buddha earlobe prank. It was not right to rub things in that way. Justine was not heartless, but sometimes you comics take things a little too far. She had struggled since the Crash, she went on, but she did not regret coming to the island. It was a fine place and would have been a good place to start a family had she had a chance to get her catering service off the ground. Still it was a closed chapter now and she was thankful she got an offer she could not refuse. It wasn't that much, actually, considering. This part confused me a little. Still it would go a ways in setting her and Mark up when they got home. Again she was sorry she did not get a chance to say goodbye in person. And she hoped I found a safe place to land. Sincerely yours, Vivienne G-H.

The second note was from Molly and began much the same way. It's too bad, etc., though towards the middle her thoughts started to jump around. She did not think our age difference would have mattered had things turned out differently. Some months ago she had stood outside my place three nights in a row trying to "mustard" the courage to ring the doorbell. Damn, I thought. Did not see that one coming. Must be getting old. She knew I was lonely. She had heard me mention Miss Muffet jokingly to Jack Spoar after class one day. Spoar had tried to come on to her but he was such an asshole with his crazy lies about his ape story. One more thing, and this is serious, she said, she did not think Mr. Kang was guilty. He had gotten a little fresh with her on the beach one night a while back but behaved like a perfect gentleman once she set him straight. She did not believe he was a killer, she said. More likely the Pythoness choked to death trying to swallow one of her mice. At least that is what some people are saying. I don't have my ticket back to Ireland yet. They are working on it for me. And generous to a fault. I think I will just take what they give me and head for Mykonos. I know a certain person there now. Molly XXXX

That was that, I decided. Fair enough. Good for the two of them. Too bad I had misread Molly. Or rather had not read her at all. Good kid—"mustard" and all. I wondered what it would taste like to put mustard on a woman's butt crack. Between her buns. Brown ballpark mustard. Maybe not too bad. I picked up a book of short stories that I was half way through and opened it. The book was a new one and the spine still gave off a fresh papery smell when I cracked it again. The stories were by a Frenchman who lived in a lighthouse on a rock somewhere. The next story was about a man who goes with a prostitute and gets the clap. He does not know he has a disease at first and has sex with his wife. He discovers he has been infected as he is taking a Christmas morning piss but is terrified of telling his wife. She is not a bad woman but she is fed up with his womanizing and had warned him, "One more time, Jules. Just one more time!" He gets medical treatment on the sly but he is afraid to make love to his wife lest he get infected again. Maybe she has the clap and does not know it. One afternoon he runs into a dashing old friend from the Resistance and tells him about his plight and together they concoct a plan. The friend will visit their apartment with a magnum of Veuve Clicquot and feign surprise that his old buddy from the Resistance Jules is not at home. They pop the cork anyway and Jean-Pierre—that is the friend's nom de guerre—slips her a mickey. He carries her drugged body into the bedroom, undresses her, and fiddles with her genitalia. When she comes to, alone, she is certain she has been raped by this Jean-Pierre fellow, whoever he really is. She is afraid to tell her husband about the encounter—afraid he will wale on her for getting drunk with a stranger in their own home. Jules, of course, wants her to confess so he can recommend she get tested for a venereal disease. And get treated if necessary. And everything can go back to normal. Weeks go by—

At my door McPheeters cleared his throat.

"Finished. Care to throw down a cold one?"

"I'm sorry, Angus. I'm beat. I really am."

"Suit yourself. Not much time left."

"I know."

"Sure?"

"Well," I said. "Okay. I'm easy. These people can wait."

I closed the book on Jules and his wife and good old Jean-Pierre and McPheeters and I set out for Aye, Claudia's. On the footbridge over the canal McPheeters stopped and we looked down into the still water. The surface of the water trembled for a moment in the moonlight and was still again. Trembled and was still again. Maybe a spot of volcanic activity somewhere in the archipelago, McPheeters said. Or an earthquake, I said. On the far side of the Moon. Don't laugh, McPheeters said. They can predict them, you know, these Insider chaps. Like the big one off the coast of your Oregon two years ago that would have taken twenty thousand lives. Can even induce them if the conditions are just right. Till the UN called a halt to their tests. The good old UN, I said. Saviors of Humanity. Something like that, McPheeters said. You ought to pay a little more attention to the world around you. I pay attention, I said. Where attention is warranted. Do you, McPheeters said. Do you really? And they are called moonquakes, by the way, my friend.

Later at my bungalow I lit up the doobie left over from the gondola ride with the deaf mango woman. The beer had been helpful but I still had an edge. There were some dirty dishes on the island counter in the kitchen and I moved them over to the sink and turned on the tap. I looked up to see if I could catch any iguanas lounging outside on the terrace in the moonlight. Framed in the window above the kitchen sink the face of an ape stared back at me. My knees buckled and this sent a jolt up my spine like a blow from behind. Something primitive at the back of my neck clenched and cringed and prickled.

"Mr. R," the ape said, in the voice of Molly O'Healey. "Can I come in? I've been looking all over for you. Hoppy said—"

XVII

I did not get Molly off my hands until close to eleven in the morning. She was a chatterer but knew how to do bacon to an even crisp without scorching it. And the scrambled eggs were not bad either. How had I missed this girl. Had Ms Grabor-Hepinstall been screening her from the depredations of an older man all along. Possibly. Too late now. At any rate, she was glad she had found the courage to come over. She had wondered if it would ever happen. She was sorry she had almost given me a heart attack with the ape mask. Hoppy had given it to her when she went looking for me at the Patio. She had told me that the night before but she was telling me again now. She wanted to make that clear. She was leaving pretty soon and still had some packing to do. She would miss me now, for sure. She had had a great time, though the mustard business was a little advanced, she thought, for a girl of her tender years. Did you do it because I'm a Catholic girl, she wanted to know. To mask the incensed order of sanity, and she winked. Give the Blind Beggar a goodbye kiss for me, she said, as she backed out the door. I hope he finds a good home in a museum somewhere. I will never forget the both of you.

An hour later a small pontoon water taxi was waiting for me at the foot of the wall. The pilot smiled when he saw me. I had to wade in a couple of yards but the water never reached above my knees. I held my sandals in one hand and pulled myself aboard with the other. Once we set off the pilot headed out to open sea but not in the direction of the sand dredger.

"We can't get close to the beach inside the walls in the daytime," he said in Korean and pointed at the expanse of water between the beach beyond the wall and the sand dredger. I could not follow word for word but got the idea. "Forbidden." He crossed his forearms and held them up and displayed a big X.

"Prohibited," I said.

"That's the word," he said now in English. "I know that word."

"A good word."

"Off limits," he said. "*Chool-eep gum-jee.*"

"Right," I said. "*Chool-eep gum-jee.*" Even I knew that one.

"*Son-saeng-nim im-ni-ka?*" he said. Are you the teacher?

"Where you from," I said.

"Cheju. We are all from Cheju. We are a Cheju outfit."

Once we were out far enough he veered the taxi in the direction of the sand dredger. It loomed large as we approached. There was already a swarm of tug boats in the area. I strained to see the beach and anybody on it but could not make out much from that distance. And the sun was too bright on the tawny sand.

Mr. Kim met me at the top of a steep set of metal steps. The paint on them was thick. No doubt they had taken a beating and been repainted many times. The good foreman showed me around the deck but did not seem to think I would find it interesting. From a couple hundred meters up everything had been tiny, but down here the equipment was monstrous and a bit overwhelming. The cutter head—rows of metal teeth set in coiled ribs of steel—on the end of one of the big suction pipes was painted bright red and had an obscene glans penis shape. It was hard to look at and not feel a little uneasy.

I followed Mr. Kim up some more metal steps at the aft end of the sand dredger to what served as the wheelhouse. It was not a vessel strictly speaking and had to be moved in and out of place by tugs. It dawned on me to wonder if it had a name. I had seen nothing painted on its side except a couple of letters followed by some numbers. Cerberus, Mr. Kim said. Because of the three big power shovels on the business end. You know about Cerberus, I said. No. Ask Mr. Jang. His idea.

Mr. Kim locked the door of the wheelhouse cabin from the inside and pulled down the shade of the window glass of the door. We are not supposed to do this, you understand. He pointed out through the big window at the beach in the distance. His English got a little better as we went along. I had noticed that with Koreans. They cannot get comfortable until they are sure you will overlook their mistakes. He removed the canvas cover on a fat metal tube mounted on a Y shaped yoke. The yoke looked like an oversize slingshot and was anchored to the metal floor of the cabin with big bolts. He moved the metal tube sideways and then up and down in its yoke until he was satisfied everything was in order. Empire State Building, he said. Grand Canyon. Hong Kong Harbor. DMZ.

He peered through the tiny round eyepieces and adjusted a wheel on the side of the tube with his finger. He grunted and looked over at me. Don't have to put coins in this one. Here. Look. The big binoculars brought the beach in close. At first it was just sand at the water's edge. I could almost see the bubbles in the calm surf. Then legs. Fine legs. A woman's legs. She was standing up but facing away. I could see the backs of her knees. The yoke held the tube firm and allowed me to move the scope up ever so slightly. I did not want to lose her. Finally her ass. A wonderful ass. A perfect ass. There is a statue near the island of Capri called the Callipygian Venus. I had laughed when I overheard a tour guide explain to a couple from Catalina that it meant Aphrodite of the Beautiful Buttocks. I crawled the scope up the small of her back between the two dimples there and then up the ladder of her spine. I peeked over her shoulder. Facing her stood two other women just as nude and just as breathtaking. They had small dimpled chins and cheekbones high and wide apart and this lent them a faintly Eurasian cast. I crawled down to check out their venereal eminences. I am a man after all. These were hairless and pooched forward a tad and nicked nicely at the apex of the inverted trigon as if an old time cuneiform wedge had been impressed gently into their too inhuman clay. Good god, I said. Look at the snappers on those babes. It was true. I had never seen anything like it. Ever. *Nakta balgarak doongie*, Mr. Kim grunted. Camel something, Mr. Baek calls them. Vulgar. Dirty mind. Like you maybe. I don't know. I adjusted the zoom wheel on the side of the binoculars so I could take them in fully from head to toe. They stood tall and erect with their shoulders thrown back. Tall people who had grown up among other tall people and known only tall people. That is what they looked like. They held their heads high with their jawlines parallel to some invisible horizontal plane like birds of prey on the lookout. A group of three or four women dipped into the water. The Insider woman from the Patio Saturday night among them, I was pretty sure. A floppy eared spaniel followed them in and they tossed a Frisbee around. Such insouciance. The real deal. I crawled the scope back up on the beach where a flock of women lounged on recliners and some others sat on a pair of large flat rocks. There was an eerie feeling of composition to the whole scene—as if they were posing for a painting. It was like some en masse life modeling session. A kind of tableau vivant. Even a pair of greyhounds appeared and got in the picture. Then that feeling vanished and they were just a bunch of gorgeous women having an afternoon at the beach. Okay, I said to Mr. Kim. You guys must be going nuts with no women of your own.

"We bring a boatload of working girls out once or twice a month. As many as we can get on the pontoon taxi. You know Rudolfa?"

"Sure."

"Wonderful dancer. A little on the plump side—but wonderful hips."

There was a sharp rap on the glass and Mr. Kim threw the cover over the metal tube and unlocked the door and opened it. A hard hat spoke with gruff but muted urgency— he kept glancing over Mr. Kim's shoulder at me.

"It is time," Mr. Kim said, "to go down."

The three of us descended the metal steps to the main deck and the hard hat went about his business.

"I want to thank you," I said, "for the tour. It's been an unforgettable experience."

"No, no," Mr. Kim said. "Not yet."

I kept looking in the direction of the beach. I could not see anything of course. But I kept looking. You could not help it.

"Follow me."

We passed through a heavy metal foul weather door. You had to step over the raised threshold to get through. The locking mechanism worked by a system of levers and a big handle that you cranked sideways. It was not a door that swung open by accident. We descended some more steps and walked down a narrow passageway between bulkheads. Down here everything was painted gray with letters and numbers stenciled here and there in white paint. The electric lamps overhead glowed sleeping quarters red but you could see well enough.

Mr. Kim stopped at a door.

"In here," he said.

Mr. Kim stepped through and flipped on an overhead light. The room was small and cube shaped—what they call a "space" on a ship. There was a gray desk against one wall but no chair and a bulletin board above it with nothing tacked on it. Across from the desk a bunk was fixed to the bulkhead and on the bunk a blanket with a figure underneath. On the floor at the foot of the bunk were two empty green bottles and a plate with a few strips of dried squid and a little cup of crusted red sauce.

"Mr. Kang," Mr. Kim said. "He's here."

The blanket stirred and the man turned his face from the bulkhead and looked up and squinted.

"*Son-saeng-nim*," Mr. Kang said. "You came!"

"I guess I did."

"We're sorry," Mr. Kim said. "We were not sure you would come if you knew the reason."

"You missed class," I said stupidly.

"On my morning walk. Above the beach. I saw some purple fez guys standing around something on the sand. Old Santana shaking his head. Tall Insider guy standing there too like he didn't have a worry in the world. I knew right off. I just knew. So I beat it."

"You beat it," I said.

"Drownded?"

"Sort of," I said.

"I didn't do it. I swear it."

"Okay," I said. "Sure. I believe you."

"I liked her. A lot."

"What happened."

"We walked on the beach. After the Open Mike. Monday night too we met on the beach. Where I left her."

"And."

"We talked."

"About?"

"She was scared."

"Scared?" I said.

"Because of she mouthed off to that Hazmat suit Alien at the Patio. The big Insider guy told her she was dead meat she was not off the island Tuesday daybreak."

"Dead meat," I said. "Why didn't she get the hell out then?"

"Nowhere to go, she said. Stubborn."

"So they did that to her?"

"Because of she embarrassed them. She betrayed them."

"Betrayed them?"

"Sure. She was in a Hazmat suit too. Getting Upgraded to Companion. She changed her mind. Degraded, she said. So she took it off one night. Too early. She was drunk, I think. That night."

"Is that what jaked her leg?"

"Huh?"

"Her leg. The short one."

Mr. Kang stared at me. "That is private," he said. "But it shrunk back. Yes. Like you seen it in the Patio."

"Of course," I said.

"Are they looking for me? The police."

"No. I don't think so."

"Because of maybe she still has my semen inside her. They will think I did it."

"I don't think so. It would spoil the lesson. To pin it on you."

"They will."

"Nobody's looking for you. There's no law here. Except theirs."

"I know about that too," Mr. Kang said darkly. "One more thing."

"What's that?"

"Her glass bowl. I want it. For the mem—"

"I will look around," I lied. I did not want to tell him about that. "I'll see what I can do," I added, hating myself even more.

"Mr. Ratner. She never swallowed a mouse. Live or dead. Not really. Ever."

I did not choose to gainsay him. Not until the end, I almost said.

XVIII.

Angry Stan's museum of island oddities was empty now. The shelves had been cleared of their exhibits. Everything was gone. Still there in the back room, though, was the diorama with its syphilitic Jack Tar forever on the verge of penetrating the female ape. If you looked up real close at the Jack Tar's face you saw that he bore a striking resemblance to Gilligan of *Gilligan's Island*. Even the bucket hat was identical with its turned down brim and button on top. Some people say he started all that. Stan had picked up the mask at a novelty shop on Maui. When a Bob Denver impersonator showed up on the island for a two week gig at the Holiday Sands with a babe on either arm—a knock out Ginger and a dead ringer for Mary Ann—there had been words and fists had flown. The impersonator was surprisingly fast and had a nasty tongue but Stan had the reach and the nastier jab.

There were chairs, of course. And plenty of other places to sit on the benches along the walls where the tourists sipped the piña coladas Toom mixed by the pitchersful back before the Crash. Stan had rigged up a makeshift stage and we had a live mike and a speaker but these were more props than anything else. We did not expect a crowd. The backpackers had left when the last guest houses shut down and their owners departed. The poets and writers gave a Last Reading at the Orion and then hugged and kissed and thanked each other ever so much for the inspiration and support they had shared. It was said Mark Grabor-Hepinstall had finished his

The Iguana Whisperer novel at the last minute and that they were already on their way to Manhattan to confer with his agent. Kaminsky was the last of the arts and crafts crowd to go. The shops that peddled their wares had thrown up their shutters on streets that were already empty. Stan had planned a send off bash tonight but it was unlikely there was enough of the old crowd left to do much bashing. Toom appeared with a bottle of white rum and a stack of paper cups and waited.

The front door of the museum was propped open. Jack Spoar and Molly came up the walk from the canal and I felt a twinge of jealousy. They were with a group of three or four others and this diluted the green poison a little. Jack had the ape mask on backwards like the old Roman god who saw everything coming and everything leaving at the same time. He was in high spirits. He had really finally put his ape encounter behind him, he said. It was just some clown in a Halloween costume. It was just like you said, Harold. Just like you said. Justine walked in with Giorgio in tow. Nobody expected them to show up. I certainly did not. She was out of her Hazmat suit now, presumably for good. It had done its job, however that worked. She wore a tight slipover sweater with a low V neck that hid very little. Ever since the Blue Hole Tour I could not get the image of a mermaid on a bowsprit out of my mind. The kind with the clamshell pasties. *I'll be okay*, I kept thinking, *as long as I never have twins*. It had only been a week since I had last seen her on the Ganymede but it seemed like a month, so much had happened. Giorgio struck up a conversation with Molly. I thought her neck would snap the way she kept gazing up at him. He certainly knew how to work a room.

"Where do I sign up," Justine said.

"This a HaHa Hole event. This is not an open mike night," Stan said.

Justine just stared at him. The three inches in height she had put on brought her eyes almost to a level even with his own. Stan was not used to that.

"It's just me and Rats and Toby and Lorcan. The regulars."

"I don't see Toby. Or Lorcan, for that matter. Harold," she said. "Do *you* have any objection?"

Stan gave me a sharp look. He had never liked Justine much and he liked her even less in her new incarnation. But it is a principle of stand up you give everyone a shot if there is room. I shrugged. Why could I never say No to her. Well, I had once, and when she came back from that ordeal nothing was the same.

In the end we drew straws. Lorcan and Toby were not coming. Maybe they were already on the ferry. Nobody was bothering much with goodbyes now. I drew the shortest toothpick and went up first. Half a dozen others trickled in and when we numbered better than a dozen I stuffed my script in my back pocket and stepped up on the stage Stan had fashioned out of shipping crates and two by four planks. Stan's Grim Reaper scythe was leaning on the wall by the back door and I grabbed that and took it up with me.

"Evening," I began. "Tonight is the last night a lot of us are going to see each other. Maybe forever," I said. "You are all leaving the island in the next couple days—"

"You're leaving too," Jack Spoar said. He was sitting in the front next to Molly.

"No," I said. "I'm not."

"Harold!" Justine snapped. She was sitting on a bench with Giorgio. He was smiling and taking it all in with bemused equanimity. "You bloody well are leaving."

"Jesus Christ," Stan barked. "Let him get on with it."

"Okay," I began again. *I guess you are all wondering what the oldest of the jokesters on this island has got to say tonight.* I tossed the scythe handle from one hand to the other with the blade resting on the planks of the stage. *Well, I don't blame you. The fact is, doing stand up here in the Museum has always been on my Bucket List. You know what a Bucket List is? That's a list of all the things you promise yourself you are going to do before you die—before you Kick the Bucket.*

Yep, even when you get old you have to think about the future—as brief and dismal as that is likely to be. But you have to prepare for it—the future. Even the future after you're dead. For example, just recently I got my Sexual Organ Donor Card. See—it's got a little cock and balls with wings on it right there in one corner—and I guess that's a little mound of Venus on a unicycle over in the other corner—or else it's a hairy Valentine heart in a wheelchair, it's kind of hard to tell. In any case, they are both smiling—which is a nice promotional touch, I think, on the part of the Sexual Organ Donation Folks.

"I can't see it," Molly said. "Hold your wallet a little closer."

"Use your imagination, dammit," I said.

Anyhow, as to my own personal future Sexual Organ

Donation. Obviously I never got THAT much use out of my glands whilst I was still alive—I mean look at me, for Christ's sake—but I'm kind of thinking I could have a good time with my cock and balls after I'm dead. And what the hell, I sure won't need them in the grave. I mean did you ever see a skeleton in a coffin with a cock and balls on it? No, never. Not even on Halloween.

And imagine if my cock and balls donation happens to get stitched on to some poor needy strapping young cocksman type Alpha male stud. Maybe even an Alpha Rock Star guy or an Alpha NASCAR Driver guy or an Alpha Rodeo Bronco Buster guy. Wow. My sex organs having at it with Alpha Rock Star Groupie chicks and Alpha NASCAR Pit Lizard chicks and Alpha Rodeo Buckle Bunny chicks. Just think of it. That would be Heaven—I mean I REALLY would be in Heaven. I mean there I would be up in Heaven and my cock and balls would be having the time of our lives down here on Earth with the kinds of delicious Alpha sluts that go to bed with Alpha dudes like that. And here's the BEST part—I wouldn't even have to talk to the dumb broads afterwards. I wouldn't have to pretend that I like their stupid fucking ass bouncing music or give a shit about their vintage Super Model Reality Show tv programs. I would be home scot free up in Heaven, so to speak.

The only thing that bothers me about this Sexual Organ Donation business, really, is what if my junk gets donated to—you know—a GAY guy. Now don't GASP. That's not a homophobic crack. Not at all. Because here's the thing. Not once in my better than five decades of life here on this earth— not once was I ever able to suck my own cock. Not once. Ever.

So why should some Joe Schmoe off the street get to suck my cock after I'm dead if I never could whilst I was still alive. It just doesn't seem fair. Not at all.

In fact, I contacted the Sexual Organ Donation People and asked them if I could have a say in who got my stuff after I died. If I could have a choice in my recipient.

But the Sexual Organ Donation gal said No. That's not possible. That's not Politically Correct. It's not Fair. We don't do that. And ya-da ya-da ya-da.

Okay, I said, okay. But anyhow, I said, who usually gets these sex organ donations like mine—after the original owner croaks? Is there like a profile or something?

And the Sexual Organ Donation gal said Yeah, they are popular these days with a certain Identity group. Capital "I" identity. A certain Lifestyle Choice.

Oh, I said. And who's that?

Well, she said kind of delicately, these days the Sisters of the Sapphic Persuasion (that's Lesbians for you Less than Massive Foreheads out there)—she said these days the Sisters of the Sapphic Persuasion are willing to pay top dollar for a man's junk—and they don't mind standing in line. They are really into it. It's the latest thing.

Wow, I said. Wow.

I mean Lesbian porn is cool as hell. Everyone loves Lesbian porn—and just think about being right down there in the thick of it with a couple of Lesbian chicks going at it with MY junk and me sitting up in Heaven and looking down at it at the same time. I mean that would be even better than being reincarnated as one of those strap on dildos with the little hidden camera in the tip.

Does all that sound fucked up? Maybe it is. Maybe I am. But I will tell you something—these days whenever I run into a stunning, knock out Alpha Lesbian chick and she looks down her long elegant Virginia Woolf nose at me and gives MY sorry ancient ass the old Alpha Lesbian cold shoulder—I just look likewise down at my Sex Organ Donor Card and think to myself: Just wait till after I'm dead, darlin'. Just wait till after I'm really fucking DEAD!

The little crowd gave me a big hand. They did not roll around on the floor with tears streaming down their cheeks, but that was okay. I had had them hanging on for the next line, and the next, and those taut moments of silence are gratifying too. I made a generous sweep of appreciation with the scythe along the stage and announced, "Next artiste!" I sat down and Molly came over and planted a patronizing kiss on my cheek.

"Can they really do that," she said.

"Do what?"

"You know. Transplant sex organs and stuff."

"Well, no doubt the rich can grow their own. But everybody else has to settle for second hand, I guess. And then they're likely to have rejection issues."

"Who doesn't," Molly said.

Jack Spoar plopped down next to us. He took off the ape mask and handed it to me.

"Molly says this rightfully belongs to you," he said, and winked.

XIX.

A ngry Stan had drawn the second shortest toothpick. He stepped up on stage carrying a heavy duty shopping bag with handles on it. Stan was not ordinarily a prop guy and you wondered what he was up to. He took a mango out of the bag, held it up, said "This is a watermelon," and set it on the empty shelf behind him where the Cyclops Glass Eye had once gazed pitilessly down on tourists sipping their piña coladas. He did the same with a second mango.

My wife Toom, Stan began, does our weekly grocery shopping for us at Island Mart. But she refuses to buy watermelons because she claims they are too heavy and bulky to lug home. I tell her OK I'll buy the damn watermelons myself. I can do that, I say. No big deal. But actually it is a big deal because I'm the one who always buys the beer too—and lugging home a couple of six packs and a watermelon or two isn't that much fun.

Anyhow a couple of days after this little tiff over who buys the watermelons we are watching one of those MAKEOVER programs on TV where they take an unhappy woman—some real emotional basket case—and make her over into a Happy One. Usually it's a single woman in her mid-thirties—a single woman who is overweight and hopelessly homely and they slim her down and gussy her up and deck her out in decent duds until everyone on the show is oohing and ahhing over the transformation.

Now on this particular episode the woman's main gripe is that her jugs are too big. And they are. Way too big. The show's

MC tells us that each knocker weighs in at something like 1.3 kilograms. They don't show us how they weighed them—but they do show us photos of her naked boobs—with the nipples and aureoles pixellated out, of course. And they are big. The way they hang down her front they look like vessels that Aliens might hide in if they were hell bent on eliminating the Human Race and repopulating the Earth with their own Alien kind. Invasion of the Booby Snatchers, you might say. So they cut her breasts down to manageable proportions so the Aliens can't use them and they fix up her face and do something about her stale, lifeless hair and POOF she is looking pretty good. Now she looks like she has a pretty good chance of getting hitched— or at least getting laid once in a while.

As we watch I get a glimmering of an idea. Toom, I say during a commercial break, where do you think the big titted lady got her brassieres when she was still the big titted woman?

Toom doesn't say anything. Just stares at the tv screen. Another one of Angry Stan's stupid questions.

Seriously, I say. Where do you suppose?

No answer.

Maybe, I say, if you called up the TV Show people and asked them they might tell you. Tell them you got the same big boob problem as this lady and you need their help.

Again no answer.

Please, Darling, I say. Please. Please. Please.

A few weeks later I am in Island Mart. I have a six pack of Blue Hole Lager for myself and a six pack of Island DeLite for Toom in my shopping bag. I have something else in there too. Something I believe is going to revolutionize weekly grocery shopping—or at least one serious part of it.

Idly I stroll over to the fresh fruit section and palpate a watermelon or two. I search for a couple of really round ones. Really glossy ones. Then casually I withdraw from my shopping bag the Super Size Jumbo Megaton Brassiere that the Makeover gal recommended over the phone. A German "Brunhilda" model, as it turns out. I slip this baby on like a harness and give my shoulders a little shrug to make sure the fit is just right. Then up with Watermelon Number 1 and into Mega Bosom Cup Number 1—and then up with Watermelon Number 2 into Mega Bosom Cup Number 2. I adjust the balance—the symmetry—like I've seen my wife do with her knockers in the mirror.

And then suddenly I feel like a different sort of creature. Serene. Confident. Even a bit imperious. Not at all like that poor lost mega bosomed soul at the beginning of the Makeover Show. Naturally the middle aged housewives in the fresh fruit section are looking at me by now. Staring hard, in fact. In awe, perhaps. Or even envy. One is smiling and hesitantly touching her own breasts nestled inside her brassiere. Another is forcing her smirking husband to look away by slamming their shopping cart into his pelvis.

But as powerful as I feel at that moment—I also feel naked—and vulnerable. And on the escalator up to the cashier counter floor one old geezer sidles up next to me and tries to cop a feel just where the price sticker of my left melon is peeping out of my bra and I am forced to deliver him a sharp elbow to the solar plexus. Men, I think. Pigs! No wonder women hate us so.

Some invisible hand guides me to the checkout line presided over by the perky lady cashier who always grasped my cucumber and onions in what I took to be a coy, flirtatious way. She slides my six packs past the cash register to the little bagging platform. Then it happens. Something I had been preparing for unconsciously for weeks now. Little shivers of ecstasy run up and down my spine as—bleep—she brushes her hand scanner across the price sticker pasted on my left melon. And then my knees go wobbly as she—bleep—brushes the scanner across the sticker on my right melon. I almost imagine my little stickers perking up and throbbing in response to these caresses. (Who would have thought bar codes could encrypt such titillating messages?)

All this as it dawns on me that not only have I joined the ranks of Benjamin Franklin and Wilbur & Orville Wright and Thomas Alva Edison in contributing something useful to humankind—Stan's Peerless Melon Transporter—but in doing so I have unleashed a hitherto unacknowledged dimension of my psyche—a secret Sacred Hermaphrodite of the Supermarket even—upon this unsuspecting world as well.

Stan got an even bigger hand. He had carried them step by step up the ladder of comic improbability and let them go in a free fall of light headed mirth. A masterful performance, to be sure, if a shade tame by Stan's standards. Almost domesticated, even. Molly went over and planted a warm kiss on Stan's cheek, this one a little closer to the mouth. She hugged Toom and bosom to bosom the pair of them grew misty eyed as they traded confidences. It was all innocence but it riled me when Jack Spoar looked after her and the back of his head stared back at me. I turned the ape mask over in my hands and wondered why Kaminsky had put such a stupid shit eating grin on the thing.

Justine had drawn the unbroken toothpick. She was not supposed to be here tonight and she was not supposed to go up on stage but there she was. Somehow I had fancied age would trump other considerations and I would close the show. No one appeared to notice the unfairness of the arrangement. Perhaps they considered it a genial way of welcoming her back from premature death. She had never looked better—never so composed and confident. Giorgio leaned forward with his hands on his knees.

So this Old Fart Stand Up Comedy Teacher, she began. Stop me if you've heard this one before. He's walking along the beach and he runs into an old friend of his. Nice gal—with a great sense of humor. Maybe the best student he ever had in the Stand Up Comedy Class he teaches in the old Selkirk Building just across the canal from Aye, Claudia's. But they have a Past. A History. He asks her how she's doing these days. She says she just got back from the Planned Parenthood Clinic.

Really, he says. You okay?

Well, she says, they have this new program called Fetal Encounters.

Oh, he says.

Yep, she says. Seems they rigged up a big screen in a comfy little cubicle for her and she got to meet the fetus she had gotten rid of the year before.

Yours, she says. Remember?

Well, he says.

Yep, she says. Everything is so Hi Tech these days. You can upload an old Sonogram now and actually get to talk to the thing. The fetus, she says.

Oh, he says. Well, how is it doing now?

Fine, she says. He's up in Fetus Heaven now. Just sort of floating around like all the other stuff in Cyberspace Limbo Afterlife.

Jesus, he says. Is it pissed off—because we got rid of it?

No, she says. He's fine. He's doing Stand Up now up in Fetus Heaven.

Stand Up? he says, incredulous.

Sure, she says. It's all the rage up in Fetus Heaven. Fetus humor.

Fetuses tell jokes, he gasps.

Sure, she says. Yours specializes in Old Fart Comedy Teacher jokes.

Old Fart Comedy Teacher jokes? You're joking, he says.

Yep, she says. They're quite funny. For example, this Aborted Fetus walks into a bar and the bartender says Sorry, Mac, I can't serve you. You're too young. And the Aborted Fetus says, I don't want a drink. I'm looking for my Stand Up Comedy Teacher Old Man. Your Father? the bartender says. What does he look like? And the Aborted Fetus says, Relieved.

Shit, he grumbles. That's not funny. Not funny at all.

Okay okay, she says. How about this one: This Stand Up Comedy Teacher walks into a bar and sees an Aborted Fetus sitting in a corner drinking a beer. Jesus Christ, the Stand Up Comedy Teacher says. Don't tell me you serve Aborted Fetuses here.

Ha ha, he laughs. That's a good one. That one's good.

Shush, the bartender says. Give it a break. It's drowning its sorrows. It just flunked its Congenital Deformity Test. And you know how suicidal kids get about exams these days! Jesus, says the Old Fart Stand Up Comedy Teacher, what is it—a Mongoloid? Hey, says the bartender, cut out the racist bullshit language in here, okay?

Not funny, he gripes. Not funny at all. We don't talk like that.

Okay okay, she says again. Here's the best one. Here's the one I like the best. This Old Fart Stand Up Comedy Teacher walks into the men's room of a bar. He sees an Aborted Fetus floating in the toilet bowl. The Aborted Fetus says, Flush me down, man. I can't take it anymore. So the Old Fart Stand Up Comedy Teacher flushes the toilet. But the Aborted Fetus bobs right back up. Try it again, man, the Aborted Fetus says. I'm nobody. So the Old Fart Stand Up Comedy Teacher flushes the toilet again. But again the Aborted Fetus bobs back up to the surface. You can do better than that, the Aborted Fetus says. Jesus Christ! So the Old Fart Stand Up Comedy Teacher flushes the toilet a third time. And a third time the Aborted Fetus bobs back up. One more time, says the Aborted Fetus. Give it all you got. So the Old Fart Stand Up Comedy Teacher flushes the toilet with all his might. But to no avail. The Aborted Fetus is still there, bobbing on the surface of the water. Well, I'll be damned, says the Aborted Fetus. It's just like Ma said. I'm a FOUR FLUSHER—just like YOU!

Justine paused and took a deep breath. Somebody clapped. But she was not done. There was more to come.

Still, the kid is good, the Old Fart Stand Up Comedy Teacher tells himself the next morning. No doubt about that. Chip off the old block. Better than his old man, even. A Natural. Has his old man's comedy gene, for sure.

He senses an unaccustomed longing stir inside him—in the very depths of his being. Slowly, gradually, unaccountably, he begins to feel—incomplete—as if staring into a mirror and nothing—no one—stares back.

Jesus, he wonders. Can it actually be true? The kid is for real? He had had his doubts. Just the day before he had been certain Janine was pulling his leg.

Now there is only one way to know for sure:

The receptionist at the clinic's registration desk is cool and perfunctory. Indeed he has been cleared to upload the Sonogram—should he choose to visit. Thankfully Janine has seen to that.

The viewing cubicle is cozy, almost oppressive in its intimacy. He presses the Start button and the fetus pops up on the screen readily enough—floating on its back with its umbilical lifeline still intact. He feels a chill shoot up his spine as he leans into the microphone.

Son, he says. My boy . . I'm sor-

Whaddyawant, old man, squawks the speaker. Make it snappy. I ain't got all day. Ma's comin' in at four and I ain't half finished with her routine yet. The poor old hag. Hardly any talent at all. Don't know why I bother. I ain't got time to help all you—

No! No! Son, that's not why—

I ain't got time for you washed up clowns. Pumpin' me for material—for gags —one-liners—shit! Teachin' stand up to losers in that rotting old Selkirk Building. What a joke! Ma told me all about it. They even hide the sign-up list on open mike nights when they see you comin' 'round these days!

Son. I just wanted to try to get to kno-

Enough!

Abruptly the screen shuts down. Blank. Dark. Dead.

GHOSTED.

The little bastard.

Chip off the old block.

We all sat in utter silence. Speechless in mute wonder. Too stunned to even chuckle. Everyone in the room craned their necks at me to see how badly the beast was staggered. And I had schooled her. Fathered her antic thrusts and parries. And now this. Chip off the old block, indeed. Giorgio was beaming. I could hardly blame him. He did not crow. Did not need to. She owned the little room. And he owned her. From the darkness outside the open door came a distant hollow *Hoo! Hoo! Hoo!*—and with that the little gathering broke into laughter and scattered applause. Stan patted me on the shoulder. He had slipped over behind me when he saw where this was going. What she was up to.

"You want to step up and close," he said under his breath. "You want the last word?"

"Want," I said. "What a funny word."

XX.

I had the island all to myself for two days. Three days. A week. Everyone was gone. McPheeters. Angry Stan and Toom. Jack Spoar and Molly. Ms Grabor-Hepinstall and Mark. Miss Soobiah. The Koreans and their sand dredger. Mr. Kang. Hoppy. Kaminsky and the arts and crafts crowd. Toby Pizzadazz and Lorcan. What's her face, Tommi, the head barmaid at the Orion. Sheila. Ruth Beth and Drago Voinovich. Brother Jeddy of the World Church of the Word and Wayan. The gondoliers. Rudolfa and Joker and his two dicks or whatever it was. Old Santana. Yumi and Veronique and Gretchen. The deaf mute mango girl and the two desperados roasting the iguana. The guards in their purple fezzes. The fishermen and the squatters and the overworked porters at the ferry slip. The poets and writers and the backpackers all gone. The Pythoness and her mice and her jaked leg long gone before her time.

The town was empty. It was like three in the morning in the middle of the afternoon. The Patio was empty. The Orion. Aye, Claudia's. The Museum. The Happy Ending. The Long Pig. The Cannabis Emporium. The Iguana Hutch. I jiggered open the big overhead steel shutter at the loading dock of Island Mart and strolled up and down the aisles of tinned goods. There was enough tuna fish and beans and chicken noodle soup and Spam to last a long, long time. Eat your heart out, I thought, Robinson Crusoe. The only survival skill necessary the ability to read the expiration dates on the lids and bottoms of the cans. Still the place was empty. Ghost Mart. The doors of the old Selkirk Building were locked. I broke open a window and climbed through. Empty. The auto dealership with its cracked show windows. The streets. The alleys. The canals. The beach. All joined the Holidays Sands and La Concha and the Majestic in their desolation.

I found a gondola and taught myself to propel and steer the thing. It was harder than it looks but I finally got the hang of it. A pint bottle of Captain Morgan tumbled out from under a seat and I took a couple of swigs. I picked up an imaginary passenger at the Patio and we agreed on the fare. He was wearing motley and a cap and bells. Tomorrow, he said, is Halloween. He was drunk and refused to get off at Aye, Claudia's. We had words. A tough customer. Stubborn. You know any jokes, he said. Jokes? Sure, he said. Jokes. The word sounded strange to me. Foreign. As if I had never heard it before. What's a joke, I said. Well, he said. A guy steering a gondola along a canal and talking to himself. That's a joke. Okay, I said. I think I get it. No, he said. You either get it or you don't. You can't just think you get it. He did not seem so drunk now. Okay, I said. I get it. I get it now. Do you, he said. Do you really?

And then the Joker was gone too. Just like that. Not so much as a fare you well. Just when I thought we were getting someplace. I parked the gondola and tied it up at the footbridge I always crossed on my way to work. With the town emptied the neighborhood seemed eerily labyrinthine now and an old childhood fear froze the streets in a menacing clarity of detail—houses and yards and footpaths without people were the natural stalking ground of predators. Lions. Wolves. Gorillas. Bears. Rocs. Or dogs, I thought. Just dogs. Torn limb from limb by a pack of neighborhood hounds. Once on my solitary walk home from grammar school I cut through a vacant lot and stepped on a length of disused drainpipe and dashed the rest of the way home in utter panic. Perhaps the iguanas were massing now for a final assault on the only human left—though the one on my terrace did not appear much bent on revenge as he watched me cross the sandy yard of my bungalow.

Inside Justine was sitting on the sofa alone. Giorgio was not with her. It was unsettling to see her in my place without the Hazmat suit. She was wearing jeans and a t-shirt with a brace of foreshortened zeppelins on it.

"What a mess," she said.

"I didn't know you were coming."

"This is not a social call."

"I didn't think so."

"You were good the other night."

"You eviscerated me, Justine. Or Jasmine. Or whatever your name is."

"Giorgio thought you were terrific."

"Give Giorgio my regards."

"You saved yourself. He said so."

"Whatever that means."

"They're going to let you stay. He squared it with the others. They think your kind of brain might come in handy here someday. God knows what they have in mind. An amusing addition to their GenesIsland or GenesisLand biorama or whatever they finally decide to call it, maybe. The women too on board, strangely. That performance at the wall, I suppose. Go figure."

"I don't need anyone's permission."

"Actually you do."

We stared at each other. She was serious.

"What have you been eating?"

"This and that," I said.

"Raiding the Patio's pantry?"

"Maybe."

"Can't last forever."

"There are the iguanas. I have Hoppy's recipe."

"Get serious."

"And the mangoes. They grow on trees."

"Giorgio will take you to the big island. On the Ganymede. You couldn't ask for a more royal exit."

"Thanks. But no thanks."

"Suit yourself."

Justine stood up. The two zeppelins rose majestically. She brushed herself off.

"Will you take your eyes off my boobs for just one minute."

"Sorry," I said.

"Do me one favor then," she said. "Just one favor. You owe me that. For putting me through hell."

"For putting you through hell."

"And for the good times we had."

"The good times," I said.

"Tomorrow morning. Be up at the Blue Hole by 9:15. And not a moment later. They're going to clean up the town. You do not want to be around down here for that."

"I see. A bird's eye view of wrecking balls and bulldozers."

"After that you will have the run of the place."

"Except for the Casbah," I said.

"Except for the Casbah," she said.

Around eight in the morning a siren sounded. It began as a low wail and rose in pitch to a shrill whine. Were they doing this only for me, I wondered. I could not think who or what else it could be for. I threw some Spam sandwiches in my backpack along with my binoculars and stuffed the Blind Beggar in there too for company. I had been talking to him more and more the last few days and wanted to give him a bird's eye view as well, blind as he was. There was still a little room at the sides so I shoved a half bottle of Grande Absente in there along with a couple of champagne minis. We would make a picnic of it. Finally I crammed the ape mask in there too. Since Molly's visit I had grown rather fond of the thing and had been glad to get it back. And after all, it was Halloween.

I walked down to the footbridge and unmoored my gondola and pushed off. Hoofing it might have been easier but once I got the gondola going it glided along smoothly enough. At the Happy Ending we debarked—that is, the Blind Beggar and me—and began the hike up the gentle slopes of the golf course. The opening in the fence was not hard to find. A column of iguanas led right up to it—just under a PROJECT REPRISTINATION KEEP OUT sign. But the first in line seemed to hesitate from stepping through and the rest of the column halted in turn. Their little front legs stepped forward and then stepped back. Stepped forward and then stepped back in some ritual of eternal indecision. Something seemed to be holding them back. Perhaps they had an instinctive aversion to golf. Perhaps they understood that a golf course does not take you anywhere. That the first tee stands just a chip shot away from the eighteenth green. And vice versa. Perhaps they understood getting bonked off a tree branch by a golf ball was no way to go through life.

Still the cart paths were familiar to me and would take us up to the eighteenth fairway without much effort. You could not miss the Blue Hole anyhow—the Ganymede hovered just above it. A couple of massive dirigible airships floated high over the town. You only realized how big they were— maybe three football fields long—when they docked at the tower inside the Casbah. Without any basis of comparison, you had no idea. I guessed they would be unloading the bulldozers and whatever robot demolition crew they had in store, but the airships did not descend. They remained up there, placid, impervious and almost godlike.

The fairway adjacent the Blue Hole was overgrown but I came upon an open patch easily enough with a clear view of the town and the ocean beyond it. It could not have been a nicer morning—cloudless, a light, intermittent breeze and the sun still in its mid morning good spirits. I set the backpack down, found a soft spot to park my butt on, took the Blind Beggar out and set him down beside me and the two of us waited for the show. I checked my watch: Okay, 9:14.

You did not notice at first as the tide began to crawl away from the shoreline. You had to blink and stare as more and more beach appeared—as if some distant giant hunkered just below the horizon were pulling a blanket of water away from a vast bed of sand and mud. Within minutes the beach extended two or three hundred yards farther out than it had ever been. Mr. Kim and crew would have been awed. Through my field glasses I picked out the overturned hull of a fishing boat that must have been resting on the sandy bottom for years. Not so far out a shark scrabbled in a shallow pool like it had been dumped there and forgotten. At least it looked like a shark. The sand stretched down and out to the horizon just as if the sea had simply evaporated.

And then the water came back. A wall of water of naked and mindless momentum like some terrible vengeance unfolding in slow motion. When it hit the town it was like the town was sitting on a low table that had got it front legs kicked from under it. The water hit the beach and hopped over the first buildings and belly landed on them and swept around everything else it had failed to hop over and sucked and spewed what it had not flattened. The Patio and the Orion were no more. My bungalow was not there. The old Selkirk Building was a desert island besieged and then it too went under. When the Island Mart collapsed my heart sank. Then the water drew back and out of sight again and minutes later as if on schedule the wave returned and fell upon the debris, pushing it here and pulling it there and dragging the mass of it into the depths of the sea.

There was no third wave. Two had done the job. The town was no longer. It had been canceled out. Erased. Rubbed clean. I looked at my watch: 9:33. The big airships over the beach descended a little to get a good look. The Ganymede overhead held steady. Down the beach—way down at the far end—the Casbah sat untouched. The waves had come in at just the right angle. Good waves. Obedient waves that rolled in and swept everything mean and trashy and flawed back out to sea. You had to hand it to Old Neptune and friends for this one.

It was too early to mix the absinthe and champagne cocktails. I knew that. And I had forgotten the paper cups anyways. Still I took a deep swig of the green stuff—just to set the morn aright. It drizzled bitterly down my throat. And then a second, deeper one for good measure. A third swig went down most smoothly. I passed on a champagne chaser. It would be more prudent to save the bubbly and the sandwiches for later. With the Island Mart gone things had taken a serious turn. It was quiet up here now that my heart had stopped thudding. I took the ape mask out of my backpack and slipped it on and wandered over to the Blue Hole and stared into the depthless azure beneath its glassy surface.

Plock. Plock plock.

The mangoes hit the water almost precisely in the center and bobbed to the surface.

Plock plock. Plock.

I looked up in time to see the door of the gondola fold closed. Indeed an accomplished bombardier.

Three apes emerged from a grove that would have been the out of bounds in the old golf course days. They held back warily and jabbered among themselves. One thumped the ground with the flat of its palm. Another gazed up at the Ganymede overhead. The third ape stood upright and strode to the edge of the water. It gave me a searching tilt headed look and plunged in and moments later emerged with an armful of mangoes. The other two apes howled with delight and slapped at each other playfully. Never before had I seen an audience so delirious with its own antics. The ape that had retrieved the mangoes strutted up to me on its hind legs. It did not look like it had much practice walking that way but I had the sense it was quite pleased with itself. It held a mango in each hand and extended one to me as if bidding me to palpate it. I accepted the gift and pressed it to my papier mache lips. The beast cooed with satisfaction and turned and lifted up its rear end and presented me with its hinder parts. It was a she—her vulva velvety and shockingly, intoxicatingly human.

Robert Perchan was born in Cleveland, Ohio, and grew up there doing pretty much what was expected of him. After grad school he taught introductory composition and literature courses aboard three different mostly seaworthy vessels for the U.S. Navy's Program for Afloat College Education (PACE) before moving on to universities in South Korea. His poetry collection *Fluid in Darkness, Frozen in Light* won the 1999 Pearl Poetry Prize and the final judge, after generously praising the poems therein, was perspicacious enough to offer this prophetic observation about the author on the back cover: "I suspect he will not be invited to the White House for Poetry Month celebrations . . ." That was like about five Presidents ago, and thankfully appears to be holding true. Beware his prose fiction in *Tropic of Scorpio* as well. The geezer appears not to have lost a step there either. Also of note: Bob's *Last Notes from a Split Peninsula: Poems and Prose Poems* was brought out by UnCollected Press in 2021. In any case, Bob continues to eat and drink and write in Busan, ROK, under the bemused gaze of his wife, Mi-kyung Lee, who has done the real work over the past several years translating novels by Jane Austen, Elizabeth Gaskell and Sinclair Lewis.

9 781956 005813